TANGLED
IN Tinsel

USA Today Bestselling Author
TRILINA
PUCCI

synopsis

Imagine being snowed in with four hot, successful men.

P.S. They've all played the hero in too many of your naughtiest dreams.

Problem is, you work for them, and that makes them off-limits.

Except now they're looking at you like you're Santa's cookies.

And they definitely want to take a bite.

Talk about making you reconsider your life choices.

These four are aiming for Santa's naughty list, and I'm pretty sure I'm getting:

Jace

Reed

Alec

...and Cole

for Christmas.

It might've started as a decorating job.

But it ended *Tangled in Tinsel.*

playlist ♪♪

1. Baby, It's Cold Outside—Frank Sinatra
2. Rockin' Around the Christmas Tree—Brenda Lee
3. Kiss Me It's Christmas—Leona Lewis
4. Naughty List—Liam Payne & Dixie D'Amelio
5. It's Beginning to Look a Lot Like Christmas—Michael Bublé
6. Blue Christmas—Elvis Presley
7. Underneath the Tree—Kelly Clarkson
8. All I Want for Christmas Is You—Mariah Carey
9. Let It Snow! Let It Snow! Let It Snow!—Frank Sinatra
10. I Saw Mommy Kissing Santa Claus—The Jackson 5
11. Sleigh Ride—The Ronettes
12. Step Into Christmas—Elton John
13. Christmas Wrapping—Spice Girls
14. White Christmas—Bill Pinkney and The Drifters
15. My Kind of Present—Meghan Trainor
16. Santa Baby—Eartha Kitt
17. Mistress for Christmas—AC/DC
18. Back Door Santa—Clarence Carter
19. Christmas in Hollis—Run-D.M.C.
20. Jingle Bell Rock—Hall & Oates
21. I'll Be Home for Christmas—Tate McRae
22. Kiss You This Christmas—Why Don't We
23. Merry Christmas, Baby—Christina Aguilera
24. Last Christmas—Wham!

 **dedication**

To long car conversations, explanatory knee-swaying videos, and Christmas puns. This one's for us, Katie. And for everyone who needs an escape during an otherwise "I'm gonna need to take another deep breath" kind of day. This is for you too.
Here's to a smutty holiday season!

dear reader,

This year, I wanted to create something fun and special for us. So I decided to provide an *"every woman"* experience. That means the heroine is not described. I did it on purpose to allow anyone reading the chance to picture themselves or someone who looks like them. I really tried to keep her as vague as possible. So enjoy, because this one's for you and you and you and YOU!

xoxo, Trilina

THE SNOW IS GENTLY FALLING.
THE SMELL OF CINNAMON FILLS THE AIR.
AS OUR HEROINE, SAMANTHA,
DECORATES CHRISTMAS TREES WITHOUT CARE.
BUT SOON, A STORM WILL WHIP THROUGH THE HOUSE.
AND FORCE OUR HEROES TO ERASE ALL THEIR DOUBTS.
BECAUSE UPON THIS MAGICAL, BLISTERING EVE,
DIRTY, DELICIOUS IDEAS WILL THEY WEAVE.
AND THE LONGER THE SNOW HOLDS STEADY OUTSIDE,
THESE FOUR MEN WILL TAKE THIS GIRL ON A
COCK-FILLED RIDE.
SO, LET'S PEEK INSIDE TO WATCH IT UNFOLD.
REJOICE!
THERE ARE DIRTY FUCKING DEEDS FOR US TO BEHOLD.

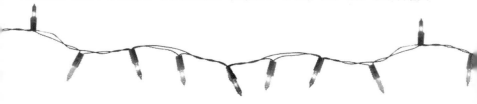

one

. . .

"Baby, it's cold outside."

Christmas music plays in my ears as I scan the twenty-foot Douglas fir. It's moments like this that make being an interior designer worth it. I've been left alone, given an unlimited party budget to deck the halls, so to speak, in this cozy yet extravagant cabin.

I smile to myself as I take in the snow gently falling outside the floor-to-ceiling windows set aside the fireplace crackling below the hearth I just decorated with holly.

If the guests don't *ooh and ahh* when they walk into this great room, I will personally pelt them with snowballs. The view alone is a scene from one of those Hallmark movies where the heroine works at a flower shop nobody ever seems to visit. But she still lives in a house outside the normal budget for anyone not coasting past six figures. *God, I love those.*

But even if my client doesn't love this—*he will*—life could be worse. Trust me, last year, I was listening to how plaid is the new gingham by a woman who lets her poodles kiss her on the mouth for way too long. They were, like, *really* in there, sorting around her molars. I shiver, remembering how gross it was.

This year, however, has set a new bar. It was *out* with the Karens, and *in* with the four best clients a girl could ask for.

I tilt my head, trying to scope out the perfect spot for the star in my hand as ringing interrupts the music in my ear.

"Hey, what's up?" I answer, tapping one of my AirPods, already knowing who it is. "I'm knee-deep in tinsel and red balls."

My sister snorts from the other end.

"It's better than blue ones."

I push to my tiptoes on the ladder, placing the star in the perfect spot.

"You're dumb. But what's up? Make it quick. I'm pretty sure Mr. Price and his associates will be back soon."

She whistles. "Wait, you're working for that hot-ass CEO again—you left that out this morning when you tore out of here."

"One, I was going to be late because the roads were already slushy. Two, I told you I was doing some fun festivities decorating for a who's-who private party. That's all the info you need."

She's not even listening to me because she keeps going.

"—And let's not forget his band of equally fuckable friends. Are those the 'associates' because I'd like them to associate their tongue with my—"

"Oh my god," I rush out, interrupting her. "I'm hanging up on you. You're so disgusting. I'm working. What do you want?"

I can picture her evil grin.

"Come on. Fess up...you've never, ever thought about it?"

I look over my shoulder before I answer her.

"I'm perfectly capable of entertaining my fantasies with the help of my vibrator. There. Happy?"

"You're so boring."

"Hanging up," I counter, sing-songy.

"Shut up. I'm calling because have you checked the news?"

I'm shaking my head as I climb down the ladder.

"No, I haven't. What about *I'm working* is so confusing?"

The sound of her television gets louder until I hear every word.

If you wished for a white Christmas, it looks like Jack Frost has finally arrived.

We're expecting a record number of inches here in many parts of the East Bay. And in Stanislaus County and its surrounding areas, we're anticipating feet, not inches, of snow. It's all happening pretty quickly, folks. Make sure you bundle up because, as you can see, the temperatures are dropping by the minute. It's time to bring in that firewood and make that last trip to the store because you'll need those marshmallows for roasting over the next week. You can see Highway 80 here, and it's already a mess —

Elle's voice takes over again as the television gets quiet.

"Don't you take Highway 80? Sam, please tell me you're done and heading home in the next three minutes."

I reach around to my back pocket, pulling out my phone. *Shit, shit, shit.*

"Sam," she presses, but I don't answer.

I'm staring down, looking at the maps on my screen. What took me an hour here already shows six on the way back.

"Dammit," I whisper to myself.

My sister huffs, "I said this morning when you left that there would be a storm. But you never listen—"

"Eleanor," I interrupt. "Stop talking. I need to finish this tree, and you need to call around and see if you can find me a hotel nearby. I'll never make it back down this mountain in my Porsche. I'm already screwed."

"Bitch, are you crazy? Forget the tree. Scram. You might not make it to the hotel."

"Can you not be so dramatic? I'll be fine. I just need to wrap this up. You go and find me a decent hotel. Please, and thank you."

I start to hang up before hurriedly adding, "With room service."

Elle scoffs in my ear just as the front door swings open. A cold gust of wind forces me to step back as snow flurries inside, along with *very* blue eyes.

"I have to go," I whisper, not knowing if she's still on the phone, as I take out my earpieces and pocket them.

Alec Price is standing just inside the entry by the oversized front door, shaking out snow from his salt-and-pepper hair as he greets me. He's only forty, but the look suits him.

"Samantha."

He always pauses for a moment after he says my name. As if he's considering his words carefully. It kind of knocks me off-balance, figuratively. Okay, maybe I stumble sometimes, but playing it cool around him is hard.

Tucking my phone back into my dark skinny jeans, I place my "work smile" on my face as Alec strides toward me to join me in the living room.

"Wow, it's really coming down out there, huh? Speaking of that fact—"

I'm suddenly stunned silent because I'd swear Alec's eyes just drifted down my frame. *He just checked me out. No, that can't be right.*

I clear my throat, trying to recover.

"Umm... I hear the storm's pretty bad—"

Oh my god. He did it again. I look down at myself in my cream, off-the-shoulder sweater and dark skinny jeans, wondering what's happening as he makes his way in front of me.

There has to be something wrong with my outfit. He can't be checking me out. It's not my usual work attire, but we're in the mountains, and it's cold. What does he expect me to wear? I open my mouth to finish, but he ignores me, speaking instead.

"The room's perfect. Almost as gorgeous as you—"

He pauses in that way again before inhaling slowly and letting it drift out, adding, "I can't wait to discover all the other talents you're hiding from me."

The gravel in his voice spreads over my skin, leaving hidden goosebumps, making me shiver. *Close your mouth, Samantha.* My lips fold under my teeth as I try to unscramble my brain. But I'm not even a little successful because all I can manage is a breathless, "Other talents?"

What the hell is happening?

I've fallen off the ladder and hit my head. That's it. This is one of my dreams.

Next, he'll tell me to drop to my knees because he wants to feed me his big ol' candy cane.

Alec motions toward the trees. "I didn't know Christmas trees counted as décor. I thought I'd walk into red plaid and holly, but this is exceptional. You're the total package."

I melt into a chuckle. "Right. Trees. Mm-hmm."

Of course, trees. What the hell did I think he was talking about? I blame my sister for her stupid comments. I'm blushing, but I keep my smile fixed as I turn to take it all in and hide.

"Well, Mr. Price, it's easy to decorate such a beautiful home. These open layouts are my favorite designs for making a large space feel cozy. And these Douglas firs"—I turn back—"are girthy, really nice to handle."

Jesus, is it hot in here? And did I just say girthy? Stop being a whore. JUST STOP BEING A WHORE.

I adjust the neck of my sweater as he looks down at me with a grin.

"Call me Alec." Our eyes connect. "And Samantha, you can handle my girthy tree anytime."

"Got it," I answer, shooting out finger guns.

Fuck me running. What am I doing? I officially hate myself. How am I allowed to be in my thirties and this awkward?

In my defense, this man is hot. Six foot four and not an inch shorter. His shoulders are so broad that it's a foregone conclusion that he played professional football. And that jawline. It makes Superman look soft. *Sorry, Henry Cavill, Alec's a better version.*

And he exudes this presence. It's not overwhelming or intimidating. More like his attention is a caress. Every look from those crystal blue eyes feels intentional, and that's sexy because it's as if you were meant to be in that exact spot at that very moment. Just for him to look at.

Alec's basically sexy as fuck.

I press my lips together because the embarrassment I'm steeped in is camouflaged by surprise as the front door flies open again. Bringing with it more snow and more men.

Gorgeous, charming rogues, more like.

That's the best way to describe Alec's friends. In the year I've been their designer, I've witnessed enough moments to solidify that judgment. They're beautiful bastards with terrible ideas and the perfect smiles to sell you on all of them.

They're the kind of men you'd happily let destroy you because it's better to get them for one night than for none at all. But that's all you'd get—one night.

From what I've seen, nobody double dips. Ever.

"Holy fuck, Alec. It's a straight-up blizzard out there."

That's Reed.

He's the blond one. But like the only blond guy you'd actually fuck.

Armed with golden-tanned skin, as if he's just back from sailing, he has the kind of looks that belong in a J.Crew ad. His teeth are so white you're surprised he even drinks coffee. And his fuck-me green eyes are paired with perfectly coiffed hair that exudes the kind of sex appeal that makes you wish he'd invite you to remove your panties. Because after a minute with him, you'd only need an invitation.

Reed's more charming than his bank account, and that's massive.

And if I remember correctly, and I do, Reed sleeps in the nude.

I found out one morning when I arrived early to start work on his bedroom.

He wasn't supposed to be home. The man stood, smirked, and walked lazily to his bathroom as he gripped his impressive morning wood, saying, "Good morning, Sammy. I was just dreaming about today."

I swallow, remembering how I just stood there, staring like I'd never seen a dick before. But, like, his dick is impressive, the unicorn of dicks. Girthy. *Jesus, let me never think that word again.*

Another voice fills the room, pulling me back into the present.

"That shitty townie liquor store only had the cheap stuff, but the good news is the party's canceled, so it won't matter."

Hello, Cole.

We've only met once. And that was enough to make quite an impression. First, there's the way he fills out a suit —he feels *severe*. That's the only way to describe it, like a character out of Peaky Blinders. Every crease is sharp and measured, created to make women breathless and men shrink.

Second, he knows it because it's clear that Cole controls all. Period. The end.

I restored a Victorian he owns across from Alamo Square Park in San Francisco. He took me on a single tour, had me take extensive notes, then looked them over before making me correct my punctuation.

It was high-handed, dickish, and so very condescending. And weirdly, I swear those chocolate bedroom eyes burned with pleasure at each reprimand.

If I'm being honest, I may have played his secretary in my dreams. Crawling across the room to get spanked by his massive hands for forgetting the comma before *and*.

After I finished the job, he only showed his approval by sending me a gorgeous bouquet of all-white calla lilies. With a note that read: *You exceeded my expectations. Looking forward to playing house again.*

Yeah, I may have that note hidden in my lingerie drawer.

Suddenly, what Cole just said smacks me in the face, pulling me from the memory I'm in. He'd said, *Canceled.*

I turn and look at Alec.

"The party's canceled? It's the weather, right? I need to pack up and head for dodge before—"

I'm interrupted by a set of dimples hard to forget.

"No need to explain, Sam. Let me help you."

Jace.

Jace is the golden retriever energy of the group. And the youngest, as in a hair under forty.

I was hired to design the interior of a house on the Bay he'd bought his mom and dad. Jace had moved them from Boston. It was the sweetest experience. They were so grateful and honestly salt of the earth kind of people. I could see how Jace turned out the way he did.

Even if he seems less polished. With wavy black hair and tattoos covering his body, he's a walking temptation. My favorite tattoo is on display above his collar, covering his throat—a set of angel wings.

However, I came to find out that it didn't accurately depict his personality.

I remember he caught me staring and offered to show the rest...shirtless. I'd turned into a Popsicle on a hot sidewalk. It didn't hurt that his nipples were both pierced too. I was blushing and embarrassed, but Jace stood on display until I gathered myself and took a good look.

It was the hottest experience I've ever had, never touching another person. He just let me walk around and lean in to admire the artistry before he said, "Now, that wasn't so hard, was it?"

Despite his hellion demeanor, there is something soulful about his hazel-amber eyes. Jace feels like a hug. One you want to squeeze you tight, so you can dry hump his leg.

Jace walks past Alec, grabs a bin with leftover ornaments, and snaps the lid shut.

"Where do you want me, Sam?"

I swallow, head foggy, before matching his smile and rushing out, "Basement."

Before I can say thank you, Alec picks up another bin. Then Cole brushes past me, saying nothing, followed by Reed.

My mouth won't work as I shift around because I'm watching strong men do the heavy lifting. Well, perhaps not that heavy. Most of the bins are empty. But it's still going in the bean bank.

They're already coming back up when I finally get my head out of my ass and walk to the top of the stairs. So I breathe out, "Thank you. You guys are the best clients a girl could ask for."

Alec stops in front of me, two steps down but at eye level. I bite my bottom lip in nervous habit as the warmth from his hands spreads over my hips. *He's touching me. Oh, he's touching me.*

As he finishes walking up, I'm gently pushed backward, forcing my eyes to lift to his.

"It's the least we could do, considering we're not letting you leave."

I blink. I'm hallucinating again, or for the first time. I've *definitely* dreamt about this part, but there's no way this is happening in real life. I give my head a shake before frowning as he lets me go.

"Say what now?"

He looks around at the others who have walked past him with smirks into the kitchen.

"It's snowing." Alec points toward the window.

My head swings to follow his finger. It takes me a moment to realize the white curtains are open because that's all you can see outside the window—white. I didn't notice as they were packing everything away for me. I was too busy sweating. My body all fired up like a cat in heat.

Fuck.

Alec draws my face back to his with a finger under my chin.

"You're not going anywhere, gorgeous. I refuse to be an accessory to your death."

I'm shaking my head, but he grins as his finger drops.

I can't stay here with these four guys...for god knows how long. I don't have a toothbrush. Or pajamas. Oh my god, what if I have to poop? I'm not pooping here. I'd rather brave the snowstorm. I'd *rather* freeze to death like the homeless guy in *Scrooged*.

A rush of breath whooshes out as I hightail it to the window. "No, no, no. I'm sure it's fine. I can still make it to a hotel. I mean...there are only four bedrooms, and I don't want to be a burden—"

My hand presses against the window as my eyes widen, and my voice gives away my panic.

"Where's my car? I can't see my car."

Reed's voice comes from behind. "Getting covered in snow, sweetheart. It's a whiteout."

As if on cue, my phone buzzes.

I press it to my ear, knowing it's my sister. "I can't see my car."

"What? Welp, it's probably for the best because it's a no for hotels. Sold out. Everywhere."

"Elle, there are four bedrooms and five people."

Oh god. Why is this happening to me? My sister chuckles because she's a witch.

"Guess who's sluttin' it up with four hot guys tonight?"

My shoulders sag. This is going to be so fucking awkward.

"I hate you."

"Love you. Get pregnant, and then we'll be set for li—"

16

I hang up and look over my shoulder. The masculine tableau staring back at me from the marble island has my heart picking up its pace.

My eyes connect with each of the guys—Cole's jaw tenses from where he's seated, and Alec leans back against the counter, crossing his arms. Jace props himself up with a hand against the counter as he pops a grape into his mouth. But it's Reed who holds my attention.

"I really can't stay—"

He gives his signature smirk.

"But, baby, it's cold outside."

two

. . .

"I really hope there's a detachable showerhead."

Music plays quietly in the background as Alec hands me a glass of wine, sitting next to me on the couch.

"Here. It'll take the edge off."

"Thank you, but I shouldn't."

He frowns, keeping the red wine in his hand. Once the snowstorm started this morning, it didn't stop. Now the reality of what's ahead is beginning to sink in. I'm stuck here. For god knows how long.

I don't even know how long it'll take to clear the road. And I don't have a charger for my phone. And, and, and... the "ands" are building. Alec gently nudges my shoulder with the wineglass.

"Take it. It looks like whatever's in your head needs to be silenced."

I frown because all my worry must be written all over my face.

"If you're worried about professionalism, then stop. You're not on the clock anymore, Samantha. And if you haven't noticed, time stopped existing a few hours back. We have days here, maybe a week, so says the county. They're tentatively planning to clear the roads on Monday. So we might as well enjoy ourselves for the weekend. It's not as if we're not stocked for all the fun to be had."

I feel silly the moment he says it because he's right. I'm not on the clock. And it's Friday. There's an "and" I should get behind.

I'm looking at everything the wrong way. Instead of freaking out about being snowed in, I need to think:

I'm snowed in at a luxury, fully stocked cabin with four hot guys briefed on the latest storm news and not sweating the small shit.

I'm in good hands.

"Sold." I smile, taking the glass. "This is probably one of the more bizarre situations I've found myself in. And that calls for wine. Also, thanks again for giving up your room for me."

Alec nods before sipping his scotch, then leans sideways, adding conspiratorially, "Guess what, it has a charger for your phone."

I smile as he adds, "Plus, I'm secretly glad you're stuck with us. Want to know why?"

My brows raise, inviting the answer, but I take a sip, hiding how nervous I am being this close to him. This is going to be my own personal horny hell all weekend.

"Without you"—he grins—"I'd be stuck with these idiots drinking too much while they try to out-stupid each other. You have no idea the trouble we manage to get into together."

My lips rest against the wineglass. The idea of them on their worst behavior is appealing. Alec winks like he's read my thoughts before finishing.

"But now they'll be on their best behavior. Unless you request differently."

"So all the fun's up to me, huh?"

I meant it innocently, but somehow the raise of Alec's brows has me blushing again. My head shifts toward the three different Christmas trees that are now shining brightly with twinkling lights reflecting off the dark windows. I take an even bigger swig of my wine, hoping it'll help me chill out before I try a new subject.

"It's a shame something so beautiful will go unseen. I'm happy I put the finishing touches on the last one once you held me hostage."

I look back toward Alec, but Cole catches my eyes. He's sitting in a high-back leather chair. His black tie is long gone as he undoes the top button of his dress shirt.

Cole was the only guy dressed as if he'd been at work. He probably had been. He seems like the type to never relax, even for a Christmas party. So serious and single-minded. It makes his whole demeanor more severe than the others.

I blink, trying to disconnect from him. But it's no use because I'm locked onto the way his tongue is trailing over his bottom lip. It's wiping up the leftover whiskey from the drink he just took. Just as I start to look away, Cole locks eyes with me.

It's the kind of eye contact that doesn't waver. The kind

that makes you nervous. And the kind that leaves you believing *this man can fuck.*

Alec's voice caresses my thoughts as Cole minutely lifts his drink in cheers. "I think everyone appreciates the beauty within this room."

Before I can speak, Jace yells my name, pulling everyone's attention toward the kitchen. Except for mine. No, I'm still staring at Cole. I blink a few times quickly. Hold on. Did I see that right?

Did he mouth what I think he said? No, there's no way.

But still, I squeeze my thighs together before jerking my head to the side, feeling dizzy.

No more wine for me. Alec said to enjoy myself, but some lines never need to be crossed. Ever.

"Please tell me you know how to cook," Jace calls out.

I narrow my eyes, ready to mess with him and ignore Cole. "Why? Because I'm a woman."

"No, because you're the smartest one here. I assumed self-preservation won out a long time ago over sheer laziness."

Reed chuckles. "*And* because you're a woman."

"Eww," I snark but still stand up, walking toward the kitchen. "None of you know how to cook? Seriously? It's a basic skill, guys."

"No. But we like to eat," Reed offers, looking me up and down.

Why does everything these guys say feel like a double entendre? It's because I've worked myself into a horny mess, that's why. Still, the others smirk. And it feels illicit

—so very fucking illicit. Or that's how I'll remember it tonight when I'm alone in bed.

I stand quietly while they settle around me, enjoying the view as Reed hops up on the counter, reaching for the cheap bottle of whiskey. But instead of waiting for another pleasurable zinger, I turn to grab for the apron hanging from Jace's fingers.

But Alec shakes his head, giving me a twirling motion as he approaches. My teeth find my bottom lip again, butterflies erupting as I spin around. His arms encase me, hooking the apron over my head before pulling it snug around my waist as he ties it. Tight. My body gives a little jerk at the end before I feel him close in—his lips near my ear.

"All done. Now be good and get to work."

For fuck's sake. Well, I guess we're all going to get food poisoning.

Because there's no way I'll be able to focus enough to make it through dinner without salmonella and E. coli gang-banging this party.

TWO HOURS LATER, THE LAUGHTER AROUND THE DINING TABLE proves nobody died eating the spaghetti I made. Or maybe it just proves that enough alcohol can kill all bacteria. Because the guys have had their fill of whiskey and scotch. But despite my worries, dinner's been amazing. Electric, even.

"Okay, so tell me, how did you all meet? Did you grow up together? Was this always a bromance for the ages?"

Jace leans back in his chair. "Alec and I played for the Pats and Niners together a hundred years ago. I was the last to join the group. All these assholes knew each other before."

I look at Alec. "You were a quarterback, right?"

He nods, but Jace huffs, "Quit fangirling. I made him look good with all my touchdowns. So don't get too dreamy over there, cutie."

Jace's faint Boston accent gets stronger when he's been drinking. I've been melting all night, even if I'm laughing currently.

They begin to spar verbally about who the real MVP is, making me smile harder. That is until my teeth find my lip because I'm suddenly picturing them in those tight white pants, helmets in hand, shirtless. I bet their skin always tastes like the perfect kind of saltiness.

My warming cheek meets my shrugged shoulder, brushing over it just as Reed cuts in.

"Remind me how you two manage our company? What's with all this ego?"

The table erupts with "Come on" and "Pot, kettle" as napkins fly in Reed's direction. He shifts his body to face me, acting like he's protecting me from the onslaught, bringing our faces closer together.

His breath is minty. Probably from the gum he's slowly chewing while staring at me. However, I can't bring myself to look into his eyes because it feels too intimate...too exposed. So instead, I stare at his mouth.

And those lips, attached to that mouth, blow me a small kiss before he rights himself, addressing the table.

"Settle down, animals. There's a lady here."

I roll my eyes, pretending not to replay what just happened in my head. But Reed turns his head toward mine, his eyes darting to my cheeks and then back.

"You realize that if I weren't here, nobody would know what fork to eat with." He winks. "You can thank me later for the things I've taught them."

There's a beat of silence before Alec chuckles.

"Don't listen to him, Samantha. He's just an Upper East Side snob. A rich prep school charmer who likes to remind us he's slumming it as our COO. See, Cole and I came from a different kind of neighborhood. Nobody cared what fork you ate with—but they might stab you with one."

Reed laughs a deep bass that makes me want to hear it again. I look around the table at the guys. You'd never know that any of them were ever unpolished. And somehow, the idea of a gentleman mixed with a little thug makes my mouth water just as much as a rich, arrogant prick.

I shift in my seat, facing Reed as he links his hands behind his head, kicking his legs out under the table. The muscles in his biceps are deliciously on display, even in the navy sweater he's wearing, making me feel cheeky.

"So you went to a prep school? Like the one in *Gossip Girl*?"

Jace grins, picking up on my teasing tone as I add, "Did an anonymous person talk about all the dalliances of your day? Was there a scandal? Did you know any girls named Blair or Serena? Were you the real Chuck

Bass, running around saying things like, 'I'm Reed Forthman.'"

Reed's hand shoots out, tickling my side, making me squeal.

"You little smartass. Do you think I didn't watch that show? Chuck Bass is a pussy. For your information, I went to Hillcrest Prep. The number one school in the country." He leans in closer, and I laugh less because his hand slows, kneading. "Yes, people talked about me as they should. Yes, there was a scandal. Because I caused it. And yes, I knew many girls. I'm sure at least two were named Blair and Serena." His eyes are locked on mine as he tilts his head. "But I never did meet a Samantha."

A coy smile blooms slowly on my face.

"Well, then, I'm happy to be your first."

His eyes say *fucking tease* as he looks at me. And he's right because that's precisely what I'm doing against my better judgment.

I shift back to everyone else, trying not to look affected. But it's hard as his hand glides over my stomach, retreating. *Damn. I shouldn't do this. This is bad, right? Right?*

The naughtiness of the moment keeps a poorly hidden grin on my face.

I clear my throat, looking at Cole. "And you? How'd you come to be in this group?"

"Alec and I grew up together," he offers, not elaborating.

But his eyes dart to Reed's hand, brushing my hair away from my face. Cole leans forward, forearms on the table. "In Chicago. Reed and I met in college."

"Yale," Reed offers with too much big dick energy.

Alec clinks the ice in his glass. "But tell us about you, Samantha. Because that's what we're really interested in."

Why am I suddenly shy? It's all eyes on me. The unyielding, completely present eyes are attached to men who look ready to hang on my every word. I don't know how other girls feel around them, but I'm dizzy. Especially now that the floor is mine, their attention feels like a spotlight. And I'm pretty sure it's making me sweat. I reach for my wine, saying, "I don't know where to start. There's not much to tell."

"Where'd you go to school?"... "Why decorating?"... "Where are you from originally?" mix from Alec, Reed, and Jace, making me laugh softly.

I bring my glass to my lips for some courage, only to realize I've finished my second glass. *Oops.*

Cole taps a finger on the table, making my eyes jump to his.

"Boyfriend?"

I don't know what it is about him that makes me feel obstinate and obedient at the same time. Maybe it's the brusque way he speaks. It's demanding. I like it, and I want to rebel.

Cole expects me to answer him first. I can tell because he's slowly strumming his fingers impatiently on the table. Fuck, that's hot.

But instead of giving him what he wants, I look at Alec.

"Berkeley. Double major in Business and Architectural Design."

Then to Reed.

"Because I like making places feel like home for people. It's rewarding."

Next to Jace.

"Born in Portland, Oregon. Raised in Northern California. San Jose, specifically."

And finally, Cole, who has the most amused look on his gorgeous face as I say, "Why do you want to know? It's not as if you have a chance at dating me....You're a client, after all."

We sit staring at each other, and I swear there's a crackle in the air. I can feel the heat behind Cole's eyes as he licks his bottom lip. I spin the bottom of the wineglass around the table, staring back, unwilling to cave first in this little battle of wills.

Jace laughs.

"Oh shit, Cole. I think you've met your match." I look over at Jace's dimples that I like so much as he continues. "No one ever gets one over Mr. Buttoned Up over there." He gives me a wry grin. "Careful. You might be in trouble now, Samantha."

Reed takes my glass, adding, "Here, this'll help ease the sting from the spanking you're going to get."

I know what's said is meant to be tongue-in-cheek, but I can't help the tiny shiver it invokes. A shiver that doesn't go unnoticed by Cole. Whose jaw flexes before he adjusts in his seat.

I shake my head to answer to more wine, barely bringing my eyes to Reed, but he pours anyway.

"Come on. The night's just getting fun. Let's see what happens when you finish the bottle. It's only fair. You're way behind the rest of us."

Wait a minute. Was that the third glass I finished before? Oh crap. I'd given myself a one-glass maximum. So it's safe to say I threw away good judgment.

Three glasses are my red flag area, A.K.A. the part of the night when bad ideas start to resemble my best life. Like my ten-second fantasy about being spanked by Cole. Yep. It's confirmed. I'm there—time to put myself to bed.

"No..." I draw out slowly, standing. "I think it's time for me to call it a night."

Grumbles sound around the table, making me laugh. Jace even boos me, causing me to slip back into my drunk alter ego effortlessly.

"Oh, stop it," I snark, pointing my finger at him, only for him to pretend to bite it. "See, this is why I'm going to bed. It's time for you boys to let loose and do whatever it is you do."

Jace pushes from the table, standing too like he's been offended, before looking at Alec. "Boys? Can you believe the nerve of this woman?"

Alec chuckles. "I can, but I suppose we just need to remind her that we're all grown men here."

Jace answers on the heels of Alec, "We could brave the snow and throw her in the hot tub."

My mouth pops open, enjoying every minute.

Am I flirting with a table of men? Yes.

Do they like it? Also, yes.

"Don't you dare," I bark sweetly before turning my attention to Alec. "I never took you for a bully, Alec."

I say his name sharply for added effect, narrowing my eyes as I do.

He doesn't answer right away. But there's something on the tip of his tongue, and I want him to say it. Badly. So

I raise my brows, tempting him to answer, but Reed pokes my waist, making me squirm and laugh again.

As I look down at him, everything grows quiet. The tip of Reed's tongue traces back and forth over his pointy tooth. There's something so arrogant and animalistic about it. Like I'm a snack, and he's hungry.

God, how does he do this—his attention feels like it vacuum-seals the space around us.

If he were a vampire, this would be the moment that I'd be like Bella and break my neck to expose my throat. Fucking *bite me* for real.

"Hey, Samantha," he says, hushed like it's a secret. "You know if you stay up...we'll show you exactly what grown men do to let loose... I think you'll like it."

This time I'm speechless. What Reed said feels sexy, but I can't trust myself because I can feel how drunk I truly am now that I've stood up.

My sister always says, "Never sit and drink because you'll fall down when you stand." It's the only good advice she's ever given me. But despite knowing I should run to my room before I crawl there, I keep horny-flirting.

"Ummm... do you play cards?" I grin, thinking, *Or maybe eat girls out in the middle of the room?*

He shakes his head as I hear one of them say, "Try again, sweetheart."

I swallow, wishing I was being led down a dirty path because then I'd say, *take turns fucking girls over the counter. I got next.*

Instead, all that comes out is, "Smoke cigars?"

You could hear a pin drop as they sit there, smirking in

my direction. Jesus, the number of dirty thoughts playing across my mind makes me a bonafide wine slut.

"Play Twister by the fireplace?" *Naked?*

Reed's fingers ghost the inside of my wrist as he takes my hand. "Stay up and find out." From my side, Jace breathes, "Yeah, you afraid you'll lose Twister?"

With my hand still nestled in Reed's, I look between them as a half laugh pulls from my throat. Because all I can fucking think about is us, nude, as someone calls out, "Left hand, yellow."

God, just the thought of it makes me let out the tiniest hum. Until Cole growls. Fuck. Everything inside me melts, pooling in my damn underwear as my eyes shoot to his. Cole's jaw ticks before he speaks.

"Stop teasing our girl. There's always tomorrow. It's time for *Alec* to take her to bed."

I open my mouth, then shut it, frowning a little at the smirk that takes residence on the corner of his mouth. *You were going to bed anyway, dummy. Why does it matter who takes you there?*

I hadn't realized Alec had gotten up until his palm presses against my lower back, drawing my eyes to meet his. I blink, staring up past his broad shoulders to those blue eyes looking down at me.

"You're taking me to bed?" I say way too breathlessly.

Jesus, throw your pussy at him, why don't you?

"Yes, Samantha, I am. The shower can be tricky. I'll show you the room. Help you get settled. Unless you don't want me to."

I do that dumbass chuckle thing I do when I realize I'm on the completely wrong page. Because of course I am.

Three glasses of wine, and I'm all for an orgy. I'm such a lightweight. A disgrace. I'm sorry .008 percent Irish ancestry, I've let you down.

"No. I mean, yes. I mean…totally. Show me the room." I smile. "And the shower. Yep." Another dumb chuckle. "Lead the way, boss."

Boss, boss, boss. They're all your bosses. Don't fuck them, idiot.

Reed releases my hand as Alec smiles behind his eyes, saying nothing as we walk toward *our…*

Oh. My. God—HIS bedroom.

Even after my inner pep talk, I still don't know what he's saying as we walk inside and into the bathroom because I'm mentally reliving all of dinner. But I keep nodding. Except all I'm thinking is that I need to get out of here by the crack of dawn.

I can't be stuck here for days on end with all the flirting, smiling, and growling. It's like one of those tests you have to pass to become a saint. I'm failing, without a doubt. Another day here, and I'm going straight to hell.

Maybe they have those tennis rackets for your feet here. I saw people do that on some documentary about Alaska once. It didn't look too hard.

I'll just snowshoe all the way back. It's like, conservatively, a hundred and sixty miles. So I'll get home by next week, but it's fine. It's fine.

Jesus. Christ.

"Samantha?"

"Huh?" I give my head a small shake. "Sorry, I'm so tired. Thank you for your hospitality and for, yeah…everything. I'm just going to crash."

He smirks.

"Sweet dreams, gorgeous. If you need anything..." There's that pause. *My body is on fire, Alec. Get out of here before I combust.* "I'm across the hall," he finishes.

He's walking toward the door as he glances over his shoulder.

"This might be unprofessional"—*now we're worried about this?*—"but I enjoyed getting to know you tonight. All the guys did. You should let your hair down more often."

I bite my lip before saying, "Thank you. It was fun."

"Mm-hmm," he hums before turning and shutting the door behind him.

Dramatically and indelicately, I melt to the floor, letting out a very quiet laugh before I reach into my back pocket for my phone.

> Me: You're a twat. You fed my subconscious dirty thoughts, and now I'm stuck here, and everything they say to me sounds like they want to fuck me. Also, I had three glasses of wine.

> Elle: Don't blame the wine. It's because you're a secret freak. Just let the flag fly. I don't know why you're so bent out of shape over the possibility of fucking one of them.

> Me: I don't know either...and that's because I'm drunk. No more wine.

> Elle: Nuh-uh. Way more wine. Get all the way drunk. And pregnant.

Me: What is wrong with you?

Elle: Fine, don't get pregnant. Just swallow all your babies.

Me: Ewwwww

I toss my phone to the bed, propping myself onto my elbows and looking toward the bathroom. I'm definitely going to need a cold shower.

"I really hope there's a detachable showerhead."

three

. . .

"Tell me I'm a good girl."

Have you ever been in a room in someone's house that makes you feel poor? Because this bathroom would be that room.

I should've paid attention earlier when he brought me in here because this is beyond gorgeous. Like excessively nice. Obviously, the whole house is the same. Still, something about how the sleek egg-shaped tub is displayed in the center of the room seriously elevates the space. I laugh to myself because the decorator in me is showing.

"I will definitely use *you* later," I say aloud, walking past the tub to the shower.

The shower's the kind with no door, just a pane of glass you walk around. So I strip, tossing my clothes on the floor before stepping inside to turn on the water.

Alec wasn't kidding about this shower being tricky. A hundred buttons must be on the wall, right below the showerhead…the detachable one. I can't help but smile as I reach for it, bending forward to eye all the options.

Okay, how do I turn you on?

I hit one decorated with three wiggly lines, immediately unleashing multiple streams from above that cascade like a waterfall.

Oh wow. Looks like owning a Forbes-listed holding company gets you tech money and fancy showers. I leave the showerhead where it is, relaxing my head back, letting the warmth drift over my body. My hands glide over my head, slicking my hair back before dragging down over my shoulders to my chest. Sheesh, even the temperature is perfect.

What an end to a wild night. My muscles relax even more as I stand there. I needed this shower.

I'll just wash those men right out of my hair…so to speak. I close my eyes, lowering my chin, letting the water run over my face. Tomorrow I'm Sober Sally. No harmless "one glass" of wine that turns into a bottle—*well, almost bottle*—that turns me into a predator.

Nope. I'm going to turn over a new leaf. I won't even know what a penis is, let alone be a person who thinks about the ones in the other room.

Tomorrow the new and improved Samantha will have never pictured how beautiful those four cocks are when they're hard. *Oh fuck.* My breathing slows as the thought suddenly becomes very specific.

All I can see, eyes closed under the water, is Jace standing in the living room. All his tattoos are on display while he's rubbing his hand over his chest. And his dick bobs, rock-hard, almost touching his belly button. *Obviously, in every fantasy, dicks are twelve inches.*

"Get on your knees. I'm gonna feed you my cock, and you're gonna suck it like a—"

My head draws back from the water, eyes blinking rapidly as I lock onto the treasure I'd almost forgotten about.

Hello, lover.

I grab the magical detachable showerhead, flicking the little lever on top, but nothing happens.

"Dammit," I whisper.

My body shivers because the vision of Jace is still heavy in my thoughts. What's a girl got to do for some fantasy action?

I bend forward again, trying to suss out what button I should hit. This is why listening is important. But no, I was too busy thinking about Alec's ass. Now I'll never get off. I'm a fucking dummy.

My eyes jump from symbol to symbol, my nose scrunching up.

"Which one are you?"

I take a shot by pressing a button, but that only switches from multiple waterfalls to one, so I try another. Nope, that's steam. The glass begins fogging up, making me squint to see.

"Maybe this one...shit."

The steam stops, but cold-ass water comes pouring down from above. I shriek, jumping back before immediately tapping another, barely looking at what I hit.

Christmas music begins to blare.

You've got to be kidding me.

Now I'm stabbing the button, trying to make it stop.

But "Rockin' Around the Christmas Tree" gets louder and louder.

"What the fuck. Turn off!" I yell, trying not to freeze to death while smacking the whole damn display.

I'm mid-panic when a deep bass reverberates over the music.

"Samantha."

Samantha? That's me. Oh my god, that's Cole.

Two things happen next: One, I scream, trying to cover my body just as Cole's eyes connect with mine. And two, he turns around just as I smack into that single pane of glass.

I know it made a sound. Like a bell getting rung. Because that's precisely what happened.

"Oww," I grunt, steadying my hand against the wall display, miraculously turning off the music and the water.

I don't know when he turned around, but I do know that Cole is rushing toward me as I stand naked, holding my nose.

He jerks me forward, tugging my hand from my face.

"Hold this. Let me see."

"Hold what? Why are you here? I'm naked," I say in one big run-on sentence. I'm gripping something soft, so I look down. "I have a towel."

"You do. Now stop moving *and* talking. I need to see if you're bleeding."

I do, in fact, stop talking as I stand there being evaluated because my face hurts, I'm still drunk, and Cole is standing in front of me while I'm only wearing a towel. The last thought makes me squirm, just enough for him to growl his displeasure.

Jesus, this is a new low for my libido. In the face of injury, she literally pushes through like a crack whore to a pipe. Yeah, she definitely wants him to lay some pipe.

For fuck's sake. Why didn't I knock myself out?

Cole's eyes meet mine.

"You're good. No blood. Now, you want to share why you were having a Christmas concert for the whole mountain?"

I stare back with half a smile on my face. Cole makes me feel like a child, but not in a gross way. In that very dominant—*you might get your grown-ass fucked*—kind of way. And although everything about this is inappropriate, his proximity to my naked body has wholly short-circuited the rational thinking part of my brain.

His eyes narrow as I say, "Because I didn't listen to the directions."

I didn't mean it to sound flirtatious, but damn if it doesn't sound like permission to make me drop to my knees. Cole's silent. His dark brown bedroom eyes search mine like he's muddling around a thought. But before he says anything, I touch my nose and grin, wincing.

"Don't worry, I won't tell anyone you were nice to me. Wouldn't want you off the naughty list."

Cole steps into the shower, rolling up his shirt sleeves, forcing me to take a few steps back before he reaches around me. He's so close that the delicious smell of his cologne makes me think I might float after it when he leaves.

"I can be nice, Samantha. You just have to earn it." My lips part as I suck in a soft gasp. "Waterfalls or shower-head, sweetheart?"

Oh, that look. Cole knows exactly what he's asking. And I'm going to follow him right to where he's leading.

"Showerhead," I say unabashedly because the fucking hussy didn't get knocked out of me.

But before I melt into him, he smacks a button. The showerhead springs to life, water shooting out all over the back of my towel, making me jump as he chuckles.

Asshole.

He doesn't say anything as he steps back, but I still stand like a deer in headlights, eyes wide, as he turns around and walks out of the door, shutting it behind him.

Holy shit. What was that? And can I have some more?

"Oh crap," I whisper, remembering my towel is getting wet before I toss it outside the shower.

My back hits the cold tile as I stare at the bathroom door. *Fuck you, Cole Hudson.* The smile on my face won't stop growing. He's just so hot. Between his presence and that asshole attitude, it's intoxicating.

Jesus, I have problems. Because I'm revved up all over again.

Casually, I turn around, acting like I'm just going to take a shower...acting for whom? I don't fucking know because I'm alone. But I did just smash my face, so maybe that's why I've lost it. Either way, I take the nozzle, glancing at the door again, before running the water down my body straight to where I want it.

There's no time to waste. My body is on fire between my Jace vision and whatever the hell just happened with Cole.

I suck in every bit of air in the room as the feeling hits me like a jackhammer. My chest immediately begins to rise and fall as I pant. I start to put my hand on the wall but then stop. *Buttons are bad.*

Instead, I press it against the glass as I rock my hips forward, letting the water graze my clit.

Every fantasy I've had tonight begins to play out in my mind. Jace, Alec, Reed...Cole. They're all there. Each touching me, tasting me, taking their sweet time to make me come.

Fuck. Me. My eyes squeeze shut, letting myself fall down the rabbit hole.

"That's it. Take it, baby. Be my dirty slut."

Alec's face is between my legs, devouring my pussy. Licking me like he's starved for the taste of me as he pins my hips with his strong hands, using his thumbs to spread me open. But as I look up, Jace comes to straddle my face.

"Open." *Without hesitation, my lips part for him to feed me his cock.*

I gasp, letting the water hit me in the right place again. My hips circle, quivering as the water pelts against my throbbing clit.

"Don't be greedy, J...she could suck us both. Can't you, baby?"

Reed pushes the head of his dick against my lips as Jace pulls out. Both swollen tips take turns bobbing in and out of my used mouth as I lick and suck, moaning against their shafts.

"Oh my god," I rasp. I'm desperate to come. I can almost feel Alec's mouth on my pussy, and I can practically taste Jace and Reed's cum smeared over my lips. The saltiness explodes on my tongue every time they shove inside my begging mouth.

My stomach contracts, fingernails scraping the glass as

I pant louder and louder, losing control, wanting the sweet explosion. God, I want to come. I'm pressed closer into the pulsating stream, that sweet sting attacking my clit as I grind, rock, and whimper, circling my hips.

"Fuck me. Eat me. Oh my god."

My voice is raw, husky, and full of desire. I'm so close...I just need...I need...

Like a siren's call, his face appears so clear in my mind.

He walks into the room, rolling up those shirtsleeves. Watching me with his friends. With a look of approval, the one I'm already obsessed with, written all over his face.

"Tell me I'm a good girl, Cole. Say it," I moan, too loudly, picturing how he mouthed it earlier tonight before dinner.

That's all I need. I come. Hard. Jaw snapped shut, eyes squeezed close. I'm greedy, chasing all the pleasure my body has to give, thrusting forward as all my muscles stay tensed.

I can barely hold myself up as I jerk, unable to handle it anymore. The showerhead drops, swinging below me, spraying the wall as I stare at the tile floor, trying to catch my breath.

Fuck, that was good.

I lean down, picking up the showerhead after somehow turning it off, whispering, "I love you," to it. Chuckling as I add, "The guys are wrong. You're the real MVP."

My head shifts sideways, my body all tingly as my eyes catch the towel on the floor.

Drying off with a wet towel... I guess beggars can't be choosers.

There has to be more in here somewhere. I walk on

shaky legs out of the enclosure, nabbing the wet cotton mess and wringing it out before searching the bathroom. But there's nothing.

You've got to be kidding me. This was the only towel. *Basic skills, guys — cooking, having towels in the bathroom, sheesh.* What does Alec do, air dry?

I smirk because the thought isn't awful.

But I'm not doing the same, so I dry myself with a small amount of dry section before wrapping it around me and opening the door. The moment I do, I freeze. Because sitting on my bed is Cole.

The Cole who wasn't supposed to be here anymore.

The Cole who left me all hot and bothered.

The fucking Cole I just moaned to call me a good girl.

He's staring at me, towel over one knee, forearm rested on the other. Cole closes and flexes his fist, and I swear my eyes fixate on the veins bulging from his arm.

"What are you still doing here?" I say, hushed, swallowing after.

Please say you didn't hear. I'll die. Suddenly I'm feeling very, very sober. Fear of dying from embarrassment has a way of doing that.

He glances at the towel on his knee. "You needed a new one."

I should say thank you, but I just stand there because before I can, he shoots to his feet, stalking over to me. Looming above like a giant fucking rain cloud.

So I immediately whisper, "Thank you?"

"Now you remember your manners?"

What? His hand bunches the cotton material in the front of the towel before roughly tugging me forward, forcing me to grab the top so I'm not exposed. Cole bends down as I stare up.

Holy shit.

Our lips come so close that I don't even register the rest of the world.

Consequences, what are those? Bad choices? Sign me up.

"You forgot to say please, Samantha." The deep gravel in his voice makes me shiver. "'*Tell me I'm a good girl*'...Please. Now, use your words, baby, and ask me nicely."

He heard. My entire body quakes because I'm turned on instead of the embarrassment I'd braced for. But still, nothing comes out of my mouth. I can't speak. All my thoughts feel like mush.

I'm caught in his spell. And I don't want out. I've been attracted to him since the day we met. His grumpy, broody silence was my favorite color—red flag. Every piece of me is screaming to cross the line.

Cole draws back, dragging his thumb over my bottom lip as he watches.

"Too chicken? Then let's start with something easier. How about you answer my question."

Oh. Shit. He's talking about when he said, "Boyfriend?"

I feel like I'm going to explode. How Cole looks at me like he's about to throw me on the floor and fuck my brains out has made me putty in his hands. Except I'm still feisty.

"I did answer."

He doesn't miss a beat, dragging me flush against him. Making me gasp.

"That's one, Samantha. If I get to the three, this fucking towel comes with me. Now, answer my question."

My eyes narrow with boldness.

"I did answer. You just don't like what I said."

"Two," he levels, jaw tensing.

He wouldn't really take it. Would he? Who am I kidding? He absolutely would.

"Oh, come on," I snark, throwing my arms up, daring him. "Sometimes, you just have to take the L, Cole."

"Three."

Oh shit. My hands shoot to the towel to hold it in place.

"Okay, okay. The answer's no. No boyfriend. Happy?"

The look he's giving me says it all.

Cole heard precisely what he wanted to hear. And that, for whatever reason, is the catalyst for my rational thinking to click back into place. Maybe because of how his head tilts as his eyes drop to my mouth. Or how tight he's gripping the towel around my body like it's about to be taken. But suddenly, everything feels so real.

I can feel it…his attack. And butterflies aren't an adequate description of what's happening inside.

So in one whole continuous thought ramble, I add, "But you're still a client, and I think we've had a lot to drink. And these are weird circumstances. Maybe we should just go to bed and forget this ever happened—"

"You're fired," he growls, cutting me off before his mouth slams over mine.

Oh my god.

I'm stunned, suspended in time, as his fingers weave through wet hair on either side of my head. But my surprise only lasts a millisecond because I'm already melting into him, welcoming the warm intrusion of his tongue.

He's kissing me hungrily without permission. Tongues dancing, our lips gliding and sucking over the others. It's what I'd imagine being pulled under a wave would feel like—engulfed, caught up, spinning at the mercy of something you can't control.

Cole's devouring my mouth. Staking his claim. Owning me in every way.

I've never been kissed like this.

He's taking from me, and I'm more than happy to give myself over.

My palms are on his chest, feeling the hard muscle underneath, my body arching toward him. Quiet whimpers vibrate against our lips with every shift of our heads because I want more.

But just as I start to wrap my arms around his neck, Cole pulls away, leaving me breathless. My lips follow as my eyes open, staring hazily back at his. He dips his head forward again, tongue darting out, barely licking my top lip.

I'm the perfect supplicant waiting for more the moment he retreats. He does it again, speaking gravelly words against my mouth.

"What do you say, baby?"

Without a moment's breath, I whisper, "Please."

Cole freezes. Silent, staring down at me. He delicately brushes my hair behind my ears, looking down with approval before his hand travels to my throat, keeping my face on his as he pins me in place.

I swallow, feeling his hand tighten over the motion. I'm

at his mercy.

He leans down, brushing a feather of a kiss over my already swollen lips.

"I knew the day we met that you'd be a—Good. Fucking. Girl."

Holy fuck. My eyes almost roll into the back of my head. His hand drops before he takes a step back, then another, eyes locked on mine.

"Tonight, you only moan my name. You understand me?"

I'm standing still as a statue. My body is overheated, full of desire, wanting to please him. To be pleased by him. And more than happy to abide by the rules. So I nod, but he winks and then turns around.

"Wait," I rush out. "You're not staying?"

Cole looks over his shoulder and smirks. "Not tonight, but Samantha…this means game fucking on."

He walks right back out the way he came. Except I'm the only one who actually *came.*

And after that encounter, I'm going to do it again.

four

. . .

"My kind of present."

cole

The door closes behind me with a click as I reach down and adjust my cock. Fuck. I was so close to pinning Samantha on the bed and eating her pussy until she begged me to let her come.

But that's not my role. *Yet.*

That *yet* has been eating at me for months.

Back to when Alec told us he'd seen her at a sex club and thought she'd be interested in our...kink.

A kink that's all about worshipping, fucking, and making women turn to putty...*together.*

Before this weekend, we'd planned to invite her to our annual New Year's Eve party and feel her out. Easy, natural, organic. If she was on board, then we'd take her back to our room and give her the night of her life. Everyone wins.

But now...between Mother Nature, all the fucking flirting, then hearing her moan my goddamn name, I'm done waiting. I want her naked in this fucking living room, spread wide for me to lick and fuck as I please.

Her words bounce around my thoughts as I turn the corner from the hall back into the living room.

Tell me I'm a good girl.

I'll tell you, baby. When I've pinned you down for Alec to rail. *Oh, fuck me.*

Three sets of eyes are instantly glued to me.

"What's with the look on your face?" Alec levels. "Did something happen?"

Fuck you for being so observant. And fuck me for having a chubby.

I shake my head before shrugging him off, walking toward the bar to make another drink. They'll be pissed when I tell them I made an executive decision to change course because the when-to-approach is the only thing we're ever equal votes on.

But if they heard what I heard. And saw what I saw.

"Bullshit," Alec presses. "Why the fuck is the front of your shirt damp?"

Shit.

Jace chuckles before throwing back his whiskey. But Reed lolls his head back on the couch, grabbing his dick.

"Asshole. You got there first. You crossed the line." He looks at Alec, shaking his head. "There's no denying it. I can almost smell her on him." He looks back at me. "Admit it, you dirty fuck. You couldn't keep your dick in check."

Rule number one: Never cross a line with a girl until you know she's on board. It muddies the waters.

"Fine." A horde of grumbles is launched my way. "Yes, you fucking baby. I crossed a line. I kissed her. So what?"

"Oh, come on. We're fucked now," Reed groans dramatically, Jace crossing his arms next to him.

I hold up a hand.

"We don't even know if she's into it, Reed. Plus, I was coerced."

I can't help the grin on my face. "She was moaning my name in the shower—"

I close my eyes briefly, drawing my bottom lip between my teeth, remembering her raspy whimpers as she came.

"—she wanted me to tell her she was a good girl."

Jace grips the back of his neck. "Oh fuck. This girl is ideal. I've never wanted someone to say yes more."

"Agreed," Reed offers, still giving me the stink eye.

Alec leans in, nodding. "I hate to state the obvious, fellas. But if she's not into this, then we're stuck in the same cabin with a girl we asked to fuck, who's on our payroll. That was the whole point of waiting until the end of the year—when her contract's up."

"I fired her," I breathe out over the rim of my glass before taking another swig.

All eyes shoot to me, so I add, "Right before I kissed her. It was worth it."

"Jesus Christ," Alec levels, but Reed waves him off.

"No. This is good. Nothing about Samantha is like the others. We fuck random girls down for a gang bang. But we know this one. We're unsure if she's an observer or ready to sign up for an action-packed cock adventure. And if we ask, then she could try to hoof it home with hypothermia rather than an orgasm."

"Is this supposed to make us feel better?" Jace interjects.

Reed smirks, relaxing back against the couch.

"The point is that it's good Cole veered off course. None of the same rules apply. Not with her. Alec said she seemed new to the scene but intrigued, right?"

Alec nods. Reed continues, "So, I say you let me test the waters tomorrow. And if they're deep, I dive in. If not, no harm, no foul."

We're all shaking our heads. But I speak first.

"No. No fucking way. That's a terrible idea. You're going to fuck her and then say, how about we invite everyone else? I've literally heard you do that. I still can't fathom why they say yes."

Reed's smile is too big.

"Because I'm irresistible, dick. But, no, I'm not going to do that. I'm going to let her live out a fantasy and then tell her I can make her dreams come true. If we have the whole weekend, then there's no other way I'd like to spend it than helping Samantha discover all her filthiest desires. Think of us like her pussy's personal Santa Claus. And hopefully, Samantha wants to be a very naughty girl."

We all look at each other, smirks blooming until Alec lifts his glass, the rest of us following. "That's my kind of present. Here's to Samantha getting her stocking stuffed *and coal* for Christmas."

five

. . .

"I think Samantha likes to be a dirty little slut."

I type out the millionth text I've written to my sister since three a.m. when I woke up. Because who could sleep after that night? I've been overthinking and watching the snow fall and gather in swoops across the sky-high windows of my room.

> Me: Wake up already. I could be dying. I kind of am, emotionally. I hate you. Not really…call me when you get this.

> Me: for context…I got a little drunkie drunk last night, flirted with ALL the guys, then kissed one of them. Wearing only a towel. And I may have invited him to stay in my room. FUCK!!!! WAKE UP!!!!

> Me: But like, he kissed me first. And he's fucking hot. But he also said I was fired. Soooo…

Me: Do you think he was serious? Shit. I have him on the books for a remodel of his Napa house. Elle!!!

Me: Oh god. I can't breathe. Wake the fuck up!! You have no life...how are you so tired?

I toss my phone back on the bed, pushing off of it to stand and pace. This is why I hate the light of day. Everything takes on a whole different dirty skew.

Last night, I had a sexy encounter with a broody alpha who told me I was a good girl. *Fuck, that was so hot.*

My thumbnail finds its place between my teeth. Because herein lies the problem. This morning, the narrative feels more like—I got too drunk, flirted with my fucking clients, and almost fucked one of them after he accidentally saw me nude.

I let out an inelegant grunt, tipping my head back before I pace again.

Oh, and let me not forget that I may have been fired so he could date me.

The last part stops me in my tracks as it has all morning, making me bite my lip.

Does Cole want to date me? No, right? But maybe. Do I want to date him? He did say, "Game on," so that has to be what he meant.

Jesus, what is wrong with me? I may have been fired to pave the way to my pussy, and I'm smiling?

Feminism...who's she?

I swipe my phone off the bed, holding it to my face. "I

shouldn't be left alone with my thoughts today, Eleanor. You suck."

Fuck this. I can't hole up in here all day worried about who I flirted with, and with whom I did...more. And I need coffee. Time to put my big girl panties on. Figuratively, because my literal panties are still wet, drying from the handwashing I gave them this morning.

I pad over to the door, pausing with my fingers on the handle because my stomach starts doing flips.

"Okay, here goes." My lips purse. *Or maybe not. Shit. Game face, Samantha.*

"I got this," I whisper again, scoffing before rolling my shoulders and bouncing on my feet like a boxer as I talk to myself.

"Everything is totally normal. And cool. *So cool.* Just as long as I don't act like a horny weirdo and try to fuck anyone else."

My eyes drop to the shirt I'm wearing as I halt my *Rocky* pep talk. Alec had left it for me to sleep in last night when he gave me the room tour. It's fine. I mean, I couldn't sleep in my clothes. Nobody will care if I'm in this.

"Yeah, cuz, wearing my boss's shirt with no fucking bra or underwear sends the perfect message."

I look back at my jeans, debating whether to put them on, catching sight of the clock. It's six in the morning. Those guys drank so much last night. There's no way they're awake. And the T-shirt is long enough to cover my bits.

So I quietly pull the door open, peeking out into the hall, seeing that the coast's clear before letting out a relieved breath.

Walking out, I'm as silent as possible, tiptoeing past the other bedrooms. From what I gathered, Cole and Alec are across from me. Reed and I share a wall. And Jace is on the other side of the house. Apparently, he talks in his sleep.

My nervous energy begins to fade as I reach the end of the hallway because it's so quiet. That is until I hear humming...*from a person*...as I round the corner into the kitchen.

And worse, it's the godawful song from my shower debacle.

Fuck my life. Back to my room, stat.

But my feet aren't fast enough because Reed's voice halts my retreat. *At least it's not Cole.*

"You're up early, sunshine."

I pivot, smiling tightly, discreetly pulling at my T-shirt as every moment of our flirt-fest flashes through my head.

"Yeah...couldn't sleep," I breathe out.

"Me neither," he says in that sexy deep morning voice guys get.

Good lord, he's in gray sweats and a white T-shirt. Reed presses a palm to the counter, resting his hip as he takes a sip from his mug.

He looks like a coffee ad. Like one of those ridiculously beautiful men that convince you to pay more than you should on beans from somewhere exotic. When really, they're just from a plant in Pittsburgh.

For fuck's sake, I'm rambling in my own head. His hotness has evaporated my brain cells.

Reed places his coffee on the counter before running his hand under his T-shirt, rubbing his chest. It makes his abs peek out.

I can't help myself. I glance as he keeps speaking.

"I kept having all these really vivid dreams. Want to hear one?"

I immediately think about the day I met him when he woke up saying he'd been dreaming about me. I swallow, realizing that I'm still looking at him.

It's only a glance when you look away. *This* is ogling.

Whatever. In my defense, those abs are like a neon sign. Or the temptation that takes hold when someone tells you not to look at an eclipse. Everyone risks blindness at least once.

"You want some?" he croons.

My eyes dart back, boring a hole into the coffee machine. Shit. Caught.

"What?" I utter, blinking too fast and unconvincing of my confusion. "No, I wasn't…wanting…I mean—"

"Coffee," he cuts in. "Would you like some *coffee*, Samantha?"

The red on my cheeks is definitely trickling down my neck. Inside I'm screaming, but outside I point to the machine and explain, "No, I know what you were saying. I thought you meant 'want some' of yours…but I got it. You can never be too safe with meningitis. Right?" *What am I saying? Stop. Talking.* "Never mind. Don't mind me. I'm all good."

I'll take awkward and socially inadequate for two hundred, Alex. RIP, Trebek.

Reed grins harder. "Cool, do your thing. I'll just stay right here." My eyes pull to his as he adds, "Since I'm partial to the view."

His eyes take me in, pulling that damn bottom lip

between his teeth, letting it drift out slowly. My face isn't warm anymore, but other parts are definitely heating up.

Don't look. Don't flirt. Just act natural.

What was I even doing? Oh yeah! Coffee.

I reach out to start making it, but my hand stops midair. Why are there so many buttons? This is the shower all over again. I half blink, suddenly feeling the warmth of Reed's body cloud my senses as he leans past me, facing me, hitting the ON button.

Discombobulated defines every reaction because the smell of Reed in the morning is almost as delicious as him last night when he blew me a kiss.

God, he's so close, engulfing me with his presence.

"Thank you," I breathe out, held hostage by his gorgeous green eyes.

Last night, Reed was flirtatious and arrogantly charming. Reed this morning is throwing off fuck-me vibes. *How many of those vivid dreams was I in?*

As Reed chuckles, I peel my eyes away, still trying to get my bearings.

"Cups, Sammy… start with a cup."

Fuck. He knows exactly what he's doing to me. And I think he knows I like it too. I sweep my hair over my shoulder, mouthing *I know* before discreetly sticking my tongue at him. But as I reach up to open the cabinet, I'm instantly reminded that I'm wearing a T-shirt and no underwear. Because it brushes the very top of my thigh as the air hits places it shouldn't.

My hands shoot back down, and I lock eyes with Reed. He's smirking.

This is exactly the situation I was trying to avoid and still seemed to manifest because my pussy is a traitor. She's literally the most unreliable ride-or-die. And she just set me up, making me all woozy with hormones that I forgot I was practically naked.

"Cute shirt." Reed smirks, plucking at my side. "New?"

The smile on my face is wholly involuntary as I jerk away from his almost tickle and face him. I can't help it—staring back at his devilish grin, I want to play whatever game he's playing.

Reed brings out the demon in me.

"Stop harassing me," I cut.

"You're harassing *me*," he counters just as quickly.

"How am I harassing you? I just came out here for coffee."

He scoffs, "In only a T-shirt. I can't be held accountable for my actions."

I roll my eyes, pushing his chest, moving him back a small step.

"Oh my god. Be a grown-up, Reed. Have some self-control."

Reed catches my wrist and my eyes before slowly tugging me forward.

"That's not what you want, though. Is it? Or you wouldn't be throwing yourself at me—"

I want to say I'm not. But my fucking mouth won't work.

He steps in front of me, so I'm sandwiched between him and the counter. God help me if I'm not holding my breath as he bends down. He sends shivers up my spine, finishing what he started, delivering his words in that fucking goosebump-giving gravelly way.

"—I think Samantha likes to be a *dirty little slut.*"

My chest rises and falls too quickly, but it's because my entire body just lit up like a fucking Christmas tree. How does he know that? And why does it feel like I'm on the edge of coming? As if Reed can read my thoughts, his leg presses between mine.

"You came out here, reaching for cups, showing your ass....Fuck, Samantha, I want to take a bite."

I just forgot how to breathe. But I know I am because the world is still in focus.

Reed reaches down to play with the hem of my T-shirt, pressing our bodies flush. Teasing my already throbbing clit.

"I can make it hurt so good," he groans before pulling back to look at me. "Just say please."

I'm frozen, staring up at him. His head begins nodding. Shit, so is mine. I don't know if it's because he's mirroring me or I'm doing that to him. Either way, it's my answer.

Oh fuck. I've fallen into Reed's dick sand, sucked into the serious hotness this guy exudes. I'm lost forever, like Indiana Jones and the Temple of Cock. Because I can't focus past the rhythmic strokes of his finger on my leg. And the coaxing temptation of his thigh for me to grind my clit against it.

"Sammy." He tilts his head. "Use your manners, or was Cole right? Does someone need to teach them to you?"

My eyes grow wide. *Cole told him about last night.* His finger moves half an inch higher, drawing circles over my thigh, making me suck in a gasp.

This feels all the right kinds of wrong.

Reed knows I kissed Cole.

Knows I wanted to hear *good girl*.

He probably knows what I did in the shower.

And still, his finger hasn't stopped edging toward my bare pussy.

"Look at you. Suddenly shy. I didn't believe him when he told me." Reed bends down, bringing his lips to my ear. "Fuck manners. You make me want to bend you over this counter and eat that pretty little ass until you're begging me to tongue your pussy."

I'm literally about to pass out. I'm soaked. Body arching toward him, already pleading. But all I manage is, "Cole told you? About last night?"

Reed grins, saying, "Who?" before his mouth seals over mine.

Holy shit. It's as if someone shot a race gun. We're two thoroughbreds out of the gate. His hand immediately grips the nape of my neck, gripping my hair as our tongues fight like lovers.

My fingers dig into his shoulders, kissing him like I'm starved as he presses me backward onto the counter. He's assaulting my mouth and driving my shirt up farther and farther. And I'm not stopping him. Because damn, I'm a hostage to this feeling and to the taste of him. Like someone taking the first sip of absinthe. It comes on strong, and you're instantly drunk.

He growls into my mouth, scrambling to grip the back of my thigh before pulling my leg over his hip. I gasp, but it's eaten by his hungry kiss as he grinds into me.

"Fuck. Your mouth tastes just as sweet as he said."

I don't know my name or what day it is. I'm all lust and need to be wielded in expert hands. Reed tugs my head back by my hair as he licks and kisses over my throat, smiling against my skin as soft mewls vibrate in my throat. But they're cut off as he drags his rock-hard cock slowly up my wet clit.

"Yes," I rasp, but it's short-lived.

Reed steps back, leaving me panting, breathless, legs splayed, sitting on the counter as he reaches behind himself and slowly drags that white T-shirt over his head.

"Someone could wake up?" I whisper, knowing full well I'm not stopping this.

"Then they can watch me fuck you."

The idea rocks my body, making me shudder. A low primal breath accompanies Reed's smack of the inside of my knee. It doesn't hurt, but it's enough to make me jump and spread them farther apart.

"You like that." *It wasn't a question.* "Your pussy's glistening." His eyes jump to mine. "Let's play and see just how dirty you like it, sunshine."

His palm settles against my chest, pushing me, forcing me to lean back. As his other dives under a scrap of shirt covering my pussy.

"Oh my god," I say, sucking in a breath because his fingers thrust inside.

"Tell me you're my dirty slut. Tell me how you want it."

My mouth is hanging open, whimpers caught on harsh breaths tugging from my chest.

"I'm..." I can't say it.

This is happening. I'm drowning in lust so deep I can't

speak. This is almost every fantasy I've had, come to life. My hips squirm, but he doesn't finger me.

He just stands there like a fucking god. Staring down at me as he slowly drags his fingers from my cunt and up to his mouth. My eyes drift closed, overwhelmed, listening to the sound of Reed cleaning me off his fingers because it's the hottest fucking moment I've ever experienced.

"Look at me," he growls, gripping my ass, angling my hips so I can feel every sensation.

He's dry fucking me. On the counter of the kitchen. For everyone to see.

"Reed," I breathe out, circling my hips as I clutch on to him.

"Don't say my name until you're screaming it."

Oh fuck. I'm panting. Toes curled. Legs wrapped around him, rocking, dragging up and down, over and over. Everything inside me tightens. The world blurs.

"Reed. I'm going to—hand…mouth."

Without hesitation, his palm slaps over my mouth. My eyes close, lost to the rhythm of our bodies grinding against that sweet friction. I can't breathe except through my nose, but I could be dying, and I wouldn't care because of what Reed's saying.

"That's it, come for me like the slut you are. You let me use you on this fucking counter, wishing Cole was watching."

I moan.

"Beg me to fuck you while Jace's cock is in your mouth? Say it, pretty whore."

I'm almost screaming against his palm, nodding my head because my body is exploding. *Oh god.*

"I'm going to fuck that tight pussy while Alec fucks your sweet little hole. We're going to stretch you so fucking good you won't be able to walk. And what will you say, sunshine?"

"Thank you," I rush out the second his hand leaves my mouth, panting as I ride out the wave. "I'll say thank you."

six

. . .

"A very blue Christmas."

Reed holds me in place as my body spasms, limbs tingling.

Goddamn, that was good.

You're so fucking perfect, sounds like it's coming from outside a fishbowl as I slowly pull from the haze of bliss. But the further I sink back into reality, muscles relaxed, body sated, my lazy smile fades.

Oh god, I just dry-humped the guy currently kissing my neck. The guy who's best friends with the one I kissed *last night.*

What just happened starts shaking me until it slaps me dead.

I fucked my OTHER BOSS.

I open my eyes blinking too fast, my hands clumsily pushing Reed's face away.

"What the hell?" he mumbles as I smush his mouth.

"We shouldn't have done that," I say over labored breaths. "Jesus. I can't believe I let that happen."

He frowns, dipping back to kiss me, but I dodge him.

"Reed," I hiss, my palms pressed against his shoulders, keeping him away.

"Gimme," he presses quietly, pushing back against my hold.

Jesus, the fucking gravel in his voice woven around the softness of that plea is too sexy. I'm instantly pulled right back in. Reed's too good at this. It's not fair.

But I say no anyway, shaking my head slowly. Knowing he knows I'm a big fat liar. Reed's eyes narrow as he slowly presses his weight forward, buckling my arms more. Not that I'm trying to actually hold him away.

But before his lips meet mine again, a loud growl attached to a yawn blasts from the living room.

Oh shit.

My eyes bulge out of my head, and of course, Reed keeps smiling, even wider than before.

"Looks like we have company," he whispers.

"Oh my god," I shoot out, but he wags his brows, reaching under my shirt, tugging the soft tuft of hair I leave in the shape of an airstrip.

Immediately I become a mess of feet flailing and hands batting in his face, urging him off of me.

"Are you crazy? Get off. Get off. Get off."

"You already did, sunshine. Or was it anticlimactic? Because we can try again, right now—"

I'm halfway off the counter as Reed grabs my waist, plopping my feet to the ground before he leans down.

"Aw, sunshine. I thought you liked an audience?"

Not just my cheeks turn red. I'm pretty sure all of me is the color of a tomato because I did say that. Yep, it's all coming back. Jesus, it's like being here made a fantasy floodgate break. And apparently, I'm trying to drown myself in bad decisions and off-limit cock.

His finger presses under my chin, forcing me to look at him.

"Don't be shy, now."

Whoever is awake is coming closer. Jesus, I can't function. My brain's malfunctioning. Because I can't stop picturing everything I just did and said. I need to snap out of it. I need a distraction.

So I pinch Reed...hard.

Enough to make him stop talking and say, "Ow," just as Jace comes into the kitchen.

Reed's still facing me, amused as he mouths, *you're going to pay for that*, blocking my view as Jace starts talking.

"Jesus, mornings are evil. And especially apocalyptic when my head is pounding. Fuck, I slept like shit. Where's the Tylenol?"

The cabinet across from Reed opens and closes as Jace gets what he needs. He still hasn't noticed I'm here yet, tucked between the counter and Reed's massive frame. I thought my heart was beating fast before. Now, it's pounding out of my chest. I can't have any of the other guys seeing me like this. This is so bad. They're going to think I'm *that* girl...a homie hopper—that's what my sister calls it.

I'm too old to be a homie hopper. I'm thirty-two. Sometimes my back hurts when I work out too hard or if I lay in one spot so long that Netflix dares to ask if I'm still watching the show I've been binging.

Yes, I am, Netflix. It's okay to have free time like four days a week. And on Saturdays. Shut up.

Reed says something over his shoulder to Jace, but I barely listen. I'm about to slide past Reed, hopefully undetected. That way, I can hide in my room again, but Reed nabs my side. His eyes tick down to the front of him, making my own follow.

No, no, no, no, no.

Forget about the fact that Reed's still hard. The real story here is that I've left a big wet stain on the front of his sweats. He looks like a human slip n' slide. Jesus, how much did I come? I mean, it's been a while, but that feels aggressive.

I'm sorry, Virginia, I have neglected your needs. I promise to re-up my Amazon prime membership and get those batteries coming in monthly.

In the meantime, I whip my head around, searching for anything, like a paper towel or a kitchen towel. Or maybe a cast iron pan to hit Jace over the head. I would rather him go to sleep for like a week than see this. He's got a head full of hair. Nobody would even see the dent.

Okay. Okay. Fuck. Am I sweating?

I look up at Reed, but he just chuckles.

I hate you, I mouth.

He pushes his bottom lip out, and it's cute. *Goddammit.*

"What's happening over here?" Jace teases, finally noticing I'm behind his villainous friend.

I swear Reed knows what I'm thinking because he's staring into my eyes, a challenge in them, before he winks and starts to spin around. I all but throw my body in front of him, almost falling, following his motion.

"Oh," I breathe out, arms splayed, a bit breathless from the amount of physical exertion I just gave getting my back to Reed's front. "Hey, you...you, Jace."

He smiles.

Jesus, Mary, and Joseph, he's shirtless too.

All those beautiful tattoos on display, along with the shiny silver bars calling to my tongue from his nipples. For fuck's sake, I've got one behind me with his dick hard and one in front of me, eyes raking down my body.

Is this some kind of sexual, social experiment? Maybe a pornographic prank show? Where producers got together and thought, lock her up, and we'll watch her either fuck everyone or implode.

Currently, I'd take the latter. Jace grips the back of his neck, stretching it to the side.

Well, maybe not the latter...

Reed traces the hem of my shirt, and a vee immediately forms between Jace's brows, making his sweet face stormier than usual. Jace's eyes fall to Reed's shirt on the floor, then to me in my more than suggestive outfit standing against Reed. His eyes volley between us before they stay locked on Reed.

"How was your morning? Wanna share with the class?"

My knees almost buckle from Jace's Boston accent peeking out to flirt with me. *Fuck.* But Reed doesn't answer. I discreetly flick his finger from my thigh as I bite my lip because the air feels like it's crackling. Why is Jace looking at Reed like they're speaking without saying a damn thing?

"So, umm—" I interject into the standoff, trying to

make the awkward disappear. "How'd you sleep, Jace? Reed was saying he had wild dreams."

Instantly, I shake my head, realizing Jace had already said that, so I snap my fingers, adding, "Crap…that's right, you said that. What am I thinking?"

But instead of stopping there, I just keep talking like the bundle of nervous energy I am. It's not every day you're standing in what could arguably be called a job site, talking to people you work for, trying to simultaneously hide your fucking cum stain and your deep ho-bag humiliation.

I should get workman's comp for this—Your Honor, my dignity's been injured, and I'll need eight to twelve months to recover.

Reed sweeps my hair over my shoulder as if he's going to kiss my neck, but I startle, simultaneously spitting more words out.

"Hangovers are the worst, right? I'm lucky I never get them. Maybe it's genetic. I can't say I've ever seen my mom or dad hungover when I was younger."

Somebody stop me. Hit me with the pan.

Jace's dimples slowly reappear as I tuck my hair behind my ears, still fucking talking.

"My sister gets hungover, so I don't know what that says. But then she just makes this amazing soup with intestines. Menudo. I used to hate it when I was a kid. I thought it was gross…she didn't make it then. That was my mom. I mean…we weren't drinking as kids. That would be weird. She's just a foodie—"

Reed leans in, whispering in my ear, "Stop talking, sunshine."

"Yep," I say aloud, nodding my head.

His arm circles my waist, making my eyes grow wider. So I try to step forward, but I'm pulled back against his still chubby cock as he grabs his mug off the counter, taking a sip before saying, "So, Jace, how'd you sleep? I forget."

I might need a bag to breathe into. *What the fuck, Reed?*

"Shitty," Jace shoots back, giving me a wink.

I hate them. Mainly because I'm smiling. And I don't even know how I feel other than amused that they're amused.

And what's also throwing me is that Jace doesn't seem to give a shit about the way Reed is holding me.

"Stop making fun of me," I say, pushing Reed's arm off, only to have him put it back.

Grinning, Jace closes the distance between the three of us, getting too close for good manners as he plucks the shirt right below Reed's arm. Instinctually, I lean back into Reed, staring up at Jace as he speaks.

"You look cute in Alec's shirt. You should wake him up so he can see."

I'm suddenly hyperaware of my breathing. Feeling each inhale and exhale.

"I wouldn't want to bother him. Late night and all," I say quietly back.

Reed presses himself against me from behind, splaying his hand over my stomach. I half blink as Jace keeps my eyes. But then he looks past me at Reed. Another something unspoken shared, he leans down, feathering a kiss on my cheek, making me gasp quietly.

"You're sweet," Jace offers, pulling away. "But I don't think Alec would mind a wake-up call from you."

I don't answer because I'm almost completely sandwiched between them. But before my mind can wrap around what's happening, Reed's lips brush my temple, vibrating sexy taunts onto my skin.

"Get Cole up too. Three's a crowd, four's a party."

Panic meets spiral. *I can't believe he just said that.*

I turn my head away quickly to stare at Reed, but the motion makes me choke on my spit. The cough that leaves my throat doubles, then triples, before Reed smacks my back while Jace says, "Are you okay?"

I'm nodding, still coughing as I grab the coffee mug from Reed's hand and down it, wincing because it's black.

"Not even milk?" I muster, handing it back to him, clearing my throat as I push his arm off me. "Sociopath."

I shift back to Jace with a plan hatched for escape.

"Sheesh, my throat's so dry. Must be allergies. From like dust or pollen—"

Reed chuckles. "Damn, that high pollen count in the winter. Its only rival—summertime in space."

I spin back around to Reed, shoving him to walk in the opposite direction from where Jace is standing, effectively hiding our version of the Monica Lewinsky dress.

"We'll be right back," I call out over my shoulder, hearing Reed's coffee mug smack the counter as I push him again. "I'm just going to borrow Reed to show me where I can find a lozenge."

Thankfully, Reed doesn't fight much. Just laughs, trying to dodge my hands as I push and shove him all the way back down the hall to my room.

"Whoa, feisty." He grins, holding up his hands as I close the door behind us. "What happened to 'thank you' and 'make me come, Reed'? I'm feeling very underappreciated."

I actually stomp my foot on the ground like a toddler, my finger already wagging at him. He's turned me into an idiot.

"You," I snap. "You're a menace. What is wrong with you? That was so embarrassing. This isn't funny. I work for you guys. And we shouldn't have crossed a line."

"Cole fired you, remember?" *He did tell him everything.*

"Shut up," I shoot back at his grin. "What we did…that thing on the counter—" Reed's still amused, making me want to punch him. "I just don't want people knowing or seeing—"

I wave toward his crotch and the wet spot.

"Seeing what? Your juices?"

"Oh my god," I bark.

But he comes back quicker.

"How about cream?"

"I'll kill you."

"Then what, sunshine? The evidence you like to be my pretty whore?"

Fuck. My eyes roll back involuntarily because I've fallen in love at first listen with that endearment. But I'm onto his trick, so I snap my fingers at him a bunch of times.

He laughs, rubbing his hands together, enjoying every damn minute.

"Dammit, Reed. Do not try to hypnotize me with dirty words. You can't make jokes like that in front of the other guys. I don't want anyone thinking that I'm—"

My mouth snaps shut because he's stalking toward me, forcing me to take steps backward until I land against the door.

His eyes bore into mine as he hovers over me. No more grin. No more amusement.

The silence grows before he reaches up, skating a finger over my collarbone.

"You don't want anyone thinking that you're into what? Let me finish that sentence for you." He traces the dip at the bottom of my throat as he speaks. "You're into filthy shit you don't tell anyone about? Am I close? Don't lie." He drags his finger up my throat, lifting my chin as he skates over it, grabbing my bottom lip. "Newsflash, I like the things you like."

Wait. What? Reed tugs my mouth forward, sucking my lip into a kiss. His tongue invades my mouth as his hands cradle my head. I can barely breathe. Kissed until I'm breathless.

He pulls away, eyes on mine. And any embarrassment I felt is gone, replaced with intrigue, like body-on-fire intrigue. Reed likes what I like? But does he, really?

Just say it. Ask… shit. No, I shouldn't.

This is Pandora's box, and nothing good comes. Except for me, if I'm on the same page this time.

No matter the debate in my head, the devil on my shoulder wins because, in barely a whisper, I say, "You like to fantasize about sharing?"

He nods slowly, my face still in his hands. The way he's looking at me, as if to say, ask more. It has everything inside me flipping over and over. *Do it. Do it. Do it.*

His lips meet mine again, softly speaking into them.

"Say what's written all over your gorgeous face."

"Have you ever?" I breathe out, sharing his air before he sucks on my bottom lip, letting it go with a pop.

"Ever what? Use your words, sunshine."

My hands grip his forearms, needing support because I'm overwhelmed. Everything inside of me is quivering.

"Have you ever shared someone? In real life?"

"Yes, Samantha. *We* have."

We? He said we. This isn't a drill.

Holy fuck. Reed pulls back as warmth spreads over my body.

He tilts his head. "Do you want me to tell you how we do it?"

"Yes," I say immediately. *Oof, Samantha, the brazen hussy, has been unleashed.*

But I'm cut off with words that still my whole body.

"Or would you prefer us to show you?"

I'm hallucinating. There was acid in his coffee. Any minute, mushrooms will begin to grow out of his head, and his face will spin like a kaleidoscope. My mouth opens and closes twice before Reed lets go of my face, tapping the tip of my nose once.

"Don't look so surprised. We've been testing the waters and flirting with you for some time. Leaving breadcrumbs for you to follow. Then Mother Nature provided a window of opportunity. We're all here. Snowed in. With nothing to do but each other. So here I am, asking the question."

I feel so dumb. I wasn't misreading yesterday. I had it right. But it was just so unbelievable. I didn't trust it. I'm staring back at Reed, completely dumbfounded, nervous… and secretly giddy.

Trilina Pucci

I bite my lip, staring at his mouth because to say I'm wet is an understatement. The minute he said "we," I was soaked. Gone are all my worries, my reservations. Nature has taken over. He likes what I like.

No, scratch that. *They* like what I like. I rush out my words, looking up from under my lashes.

"So when Cole said, *game on* last night...he meant fucking me was the game."

"Only if you want to play."

I open my mouth because I have a thousand questions, but he grins, putting two fingers over my lips.

"No more talking."

"Okay," I mumble, tasting a hint of myself on them.

But I'm possessed, emboldened by this new information, and turned on, so I test the waters, still following the rules, slowly running my tongue between the seam of his fingers.

He takes a deep appreciative inhale before he grabs my jaw, halting me, and rumbles out his words.

"Such a brat. I hope Cole gets to turn that ass red."

I shiver. If I've died, or this *is* an acid trip, mother may I never leave. He hums his approval as I stay in place.

"Consider this your formal offer, Samantha. If you don't want to accept, we'll never touch you. And if you never want to see us again, we'll replace ourselves in your book with equally enthusiastic clients. But if you want this—one weekend, no strings attached—it'll always be our secret. Make no mistake, *you* are our biggest wish, so no *you* will make for a very blue Christmas."

One weekend. No strings attached. *Unless they're*

74

wrapped around my wrist. Can I do this? I know I want to, but am I brave enough to try?

"And if I do…want to be your present?"

"Then come out unwrapped"—his hand drops, fingers ducking under my shirt running through the hairs of my pussy—"just like this. In this T-shirt. And kiss me under the mistletoe. Then be ready because, sunshine, we really want a toy we can play with."

Reed steps back, leaving me overheated. I move to the side, nodding, letting him pass me to the door. His head shifts to look at me before he goes.

"You still want my pants, sunshine?"

I smile in answer, holding out my hand, palm up, staring at the floor.

Reed hooks his fingers around the waistband of his sweats, tugging them off. Exposing his bare ass.

"Oh my god," I say, laughing.

He tosses them to me, grabbing his junk to cover it as he opens the door.

"Wait, you're going out there naked?"

"Don't worry about it. They've seen my ass plenty."

He leaves me standing by the door, mouth almost on the floor, as another laugh escapes. What the fuck just happened? And am I about to get railed like some kind of dirty porn starring Mrs. Claus and her elves?

Maybe. Definitely. *Ho, ho, ho.*

seven

. . .

"Cut to the chase, Reed."

reed

Her door closes as I slip out, turning around slowly. Until I'm halted by a familiar grumble. "Why the fuck are you standing outside her door with your cock out? This is you testing the waters?"

The grin on my face grows.

Cole's standing across from me, arms crossed, looking like he's about to rip my head off my shoulders.

"Don't get your panties in a ruffle, princess. Especially since *she* wasn't wearing any."

His jaw tenses before he says, "Don't push me."

But I chuckle.

"Settle down. She'll hear us." My voice lowers, "Since you're being so patient, I'll tell you. I'm naked because our girl wanted to keep my sweats. Probably as a memento. She came all over the front of them. Now, if you'll excuse me. It's cold. Wouldn't want her walking out here and getting the wrong impression."

I glance down at my hand, barely covering my dick, and wink, adding, "Seeing as she's contemplating our offer."

Cole reaches out, slapping my cheek playfully as I dodge it.

"You prick. I can't believe you did it. What did you say?"

I motion my head for us to move, but he raises his brows. So I keep my voice quiet.

"It's not a done deal yet, so don't celebrate. You'll jinx the pussy. But it's ninety-eight percent wrapped up. Nice and neat, with a little bow."

He's frowning. Then again, he's always frowning, so I roll my eyes.

"Can I go to my room now, Dad? Considering my cock is out, in my fucking hand."

He opens his mouth, but whatever he's going to say is cut off by a scream. A really loud shriek. Then laughter. All from behind Samantha's door.

Our eyes connect for seconds before we scramble, shamelessly pressing our ears to the wood. *While I'm still holding my wood.*

I scoot in closer, angling my body, straining to hear, but Cole smacks my shoulder, mouthing, *Don't touch me with your dick.*

So I return the sentiment, mouthing, *I'll make you suck it* before we get serious, trying to hear what she's saying. There's a voice I don't recognize. Maybe a friend? All I hear is a lot of laughing, so it's hard to make out what's being said.

But then words break through, crystal fucking clear.

Cole's and my eyes connect because I know what I heard, and fuck me if he didn't hear the same. We both pull away from the door. A smirk on my face matches his.

"Kitchen," he whispers. "You can give the good news."

I slide into my room, grabbing some new sweats as I picture her walking out like I told her in Alec's shirt. Bare underneath, ready for us. *Fuck.* I have a feeling watching them tear her apart will cause me to blow my load before I'm even buried inside her pussy.

Damn. I'm getting hard thinking about it. I look down.

"Rest now. Your time to shine is coming."

Letting out a breath, I head back out, adjusting myself as I join the guys in the kitchen.

Attentive doesn't quite define the way Alec and Jace are looking at me. But not Cole because he heard what I did.

God, I love this part—the anticipation. The fucking adrenaline rush of the chase. This is why I do this. That and I get to do dirty shit to willing women.

"Speak," Cole barks. "Or they might kill you."

I grab a coffee mug, making a new coffee for myself as I smirk.

"First, our girl is so fucking ready to be railed. Every dirty thing I said, she was dripping. She followed me right down the rabbit hole. No, scratch that, not followed. She led the way."

Jace exhales audibly before he speaks. "She was definitely turned on. I thought her nipples would cut through her shirt when she was sandwiched between us. They were so fucking hard. But it was how she looked up at me...a mix of curiosity and sin. That shit had me wanting to drop to my knees and worship at the altar of *her*."

Cole looks at me. "Cut to the chase, Reed. Tell them the good part."

The steam sounds quietly in the background as my cappuccino foams.

"I'm getting there. So, she's contemplating our offer. But Alec nailed it. She's definitely a newbie. I'm sure she'll have so many questions."

Alec smirks. "Then we'll answer every single one. Her comfort becomes our priority."

We're all nodding as Cole says, "Exactly. But if we do this, we're breaking our one-night rule. Everyone good with that?"

We look around at each other. That's been a hard line for us. We never do more than one night, but this is an opportunity I can't pass up, and I know they feel the same.

"I'm good with it," I say, Jace and Alec on my heels with their agreeance.

What's the worst that can happen? It's not like anyone's falling in love.

Cole raises his brows, staring at me. "Now, are you going to tell them the fucking good part?"

Jace's head swings to mine. "If you don't spit it out, I'll fucking bury you out in the snow. And Alec will help."

I chuckle, taking a sip of my coffee.

"Okay...you see...that Bonnie"—I motion to Cole—"and this Clyde just sank to a new low and eavesdropped on her conversation in which she told her friend she was going for it."

Women always think men are broody, serious, and never excited. But if someone were to peep through our window, they'd see four grown men celebrating like they'd scored a touchdown.

Make that three men. Cole's just leaned back against the counter, face turned in the direction of the hall. And everyone says I'm single-minded.

But I already know what he's thinking. Cole wants her stripped bare in the middle of the room. Christmas lights spotlight her body, so he can conduct the orgasmic symphony only sexual maestros can hear.

And I can't wait to be the instrument he uses.

"How will we know when she says yes? You always make them do something to seal the deal," Alec muses.

I bite my bottom lip before I speak.

"I told her to meet me in the living room, in your fucking shirt, nothing underneath, and kiss me under the mistletoe."

Jace laughs. "You're the most dramatic fucking person I've ever known."

"When?" Cole grinds in that *patience isn't my virtue* way.

But I frown because, shit, I didn't give a when. *Fuck me.* She could be in there all day.

"Reed," Alec groans, seeing the realization written all over my face.

Cole shakes his head, but I shrug.

"Who cares about the wait? She's worth it. Trust me, she tastes like divinity. Purrs for every degrading word.

She soaked my fingers, and it only tempted me more when I licked her clean off."

The silence in the kitchen is thick with desire. My fuckup long forgotten. Because now that we know she's saying yes, we're animals focused on our piece.

"What did she look like when she came?" Alec says, barely restrained.

My eyes shift to his, knowing he'll be picturing what I say.

"Like she was missing a hand around her throat. A cock in her mouth. And someone to watch her pussy chokehold my fingers."

Cole exhales hard before he looks straight at me.

"If that girl doesn't come out in the next hour, I'm setting this fucking cabin on fire to make her."

eight

. . .

"This is like a once-in-a-lifetime opportunity to
jingle your bells."

I toss Reed's sweats on my bed as soon as the door
clicks before running to the nightstand to grab my
phone. I've never hit a call button so quickly.

You better fucking wake up, Eleanor. I press the cell to my
ear, my fingers tapping against my leg as more ringing
sounds with no answer.

"Come on," I groan, about to hang up when a groggy
"Hello" drifts through.

Yes. My voice is more high-pitched than usual.

"Oh my god, where the fuck have you been my whole
life?" I dash into the bathroom and close the door before
turning on the faucet. "I need you awake for this conversation. Open your eyes and stand up. Yeah...get alert."

"What is wrong with you? Is that water in the background? I was sleeping, you lunatic. This better be an
emergency."

"It is. And yes, it's water. I need to make sure nobody
hears me."

Sheets rustle in the background like she's sitting up. "Are you high? You know you can't smoke weed, dork. You get paranoid."

"Eleanor," I snap. "Focus. It's seven o'clock in the morning. Why would I be high?"

She yawns.

"I mean, technically, I'm probably still high."

I don't have time for this. I'm about to explode. So I blurt out everything in the fastest run-together sentence of my life.

"I-kissed-Cole-last-night-and-then-dry-humped-his-best-friend-in-the-kitchen-before-he-told-me-they-want-to-share-me."

I suck in a deep breath. But there's nothing. No answer. Just silence. Then more silence.

"Hello?" I whisper, but she screams, "SHUT THE FUCK UP!"

I have to pull the phone from my ear, but I'm laughing. Maybe it's hysterical laughter but whatever. I put my phone on speaker as I pace.

"Eleanor, it hasn't even been twenty-four hours, and I've got two down, two to go. I'm a fucking predator. I manifested this. Or you did with all that bullshit you talked."

She's breathless, laughing her words out, and too excited to give good advice.

"Tell me you're going to do it. I will literally never speak to you again if faced with this offer. To fuck four of the hottest guys the baby Jesus ever made, and you say no. Like, I might actually hate your guts. You could do this for all of us. This is for the sisterhood."

"Not wanting to sleep with four *practically* strangers at the same time does not make you a loser. But yeah, I mean, who am I to neglect the sisterhood? I got you."

She screams again. And I cover my mouth to mute my laugh.

"Holy shit! I knew it. My sister's a dirty slut. Weirdly, this might be the first time I've respected you."

"Fuck you."

"Just kidding. Okay, okay...let's calm down. We need to analyze this."

We both take a deep breath before I laugh again.

"Sorry. I just...this is crazy, right? What am I doing?"

I hop up onto the counter, sitting criss-cross on the marble as she answers.

"Bitch, this is like a once-in-a-lifetime opportunity to jingle your bells. You'd be nuts not to say yes."

My shoulders shake as my teeth find the inside of my cheek. "Here's the thing, what if I don't have the nerve to follow through? I mean, fantasizing is one thing. They want to fuck me for real."

"Do you trust them? I mean, I know you only know them professionally, but...?"

My brows pull together as I stare at nothing in particular, thinking about what she said until I nod.

"I do trust them. They've always been respectful of me. They're not weirdos, just sexually adventurous. And I'm comfortable with their offer of this weekend, no strings attached. But I guess what I mean is that I'm out of my depth. I've only seen this go down. I've never been a part of it. I'm great in bed, trust me. But this is that meme with all the hot dogs flying at your face."

"Wait. One. Damn. Minute."

Fuck. I didn't mean to say that.

"Samantha Gabriella Thomas. You better clarify that statement"—her voice raises—"or I'm calling Mom and telling her you're getting Eiffel Towered. And that you're not even in Paris."

I narrow my eyes even though she can't see me. And I'm already off the countertop.

"Tell her," I challenge, huffing a laugh, "and I'll tell her that you only go to church because you're trying to fuck the priest after you read about it happening in some fucking romance book."

"Ohhhhhh…" The word is drawn out like the line of battle. "Low blow. That book is fucking spiritual self-care."

I kick the air, barking, "Listen." We both chuckle because we're equally as looney. "Don't fuck with me. I'm older by design. God only chooses his champions for this job. Now…if I tell you…you have to promise on Puffy not to tell."

Making my sister swear on the poodle our parents took "to a big farm where he could run free" when we were kids is the most serious form of secret keeping. Even now. You don't break a promise on Puffy. Ever.

That shit was traumatic.

"Oh shit." She answers in a more serious tone, "I swear it. They could cut out my tongue; I swear I'll never tell. Whatever you did goes to the grave like Puff-Puff."

"Elle," I level, shaking my head. "If your tongue is cut out, you can't speak anyway."

Her tongue clicks against the roof of her mouth before she says, "Whatever. You get the point. Spill it."

She really is still high.

I bite down, tensing my jaw, staring at myself in the mirror before I close my eyes and just say it.

"Remember last month when I booked a remodel of that club in Chicago? I was super excited because it was the first commercial job I got."

"Yeah…" she says nervously.

"It was a sex club. Called Church."

"Oh. My. Fucking. God."

I shush her, continuing, "I didn't do anything. I just watched. But there was this woman who walked into a room. Like a viewing room. Three guys walked in after. And yeah, they…uh, you know."

"So you just watched them fuck her brains out? Wow."

"Don't judge me."

She scoffs.

"Oh my god. Shut your mouth. Who am I to judge? Do you know how much *strange* I've had? My life is an array of unknown twat and cock. I think it's fucking awesome that you're opening your mind and finding what you want. And now you can actually try it out. But just for the record—is this what you want? Like tomorrow when the hype wears off? Because I know you…you're already internally deep diving into a hypothetical Q&A sesh."

She's so right. I do have unanswered questions, but I knew exactly what I wanted the night I watched that woman get worshipped. It was an out-of-body experience. I thought it would just get locked away as a fantasy, but now, these guys—ones I'm very much attracted to—like what I like. I want to do this. Take the plunge.

"Yeah. I'm sure. I'm doing this."

"Then stop worrying about what to do. You know what to do with one dick. Plus, men are simple, like spit on it, moan...call them daddy, you're all good."

I chuckle. "You're truly warped. It's not about me turning them on...I'm saying this is four *pee-nigh*. And I only have three hol—"

She cuts off anything else I'm about to say because that cackle of hers is back.

"One, don't ever say any variation of the word *penis*. It sounds skinny. And two, I fucking hoped you waxed those holes before you went. If not, find a razor because you look like a Wookie before appointments."

"I hate you. I'm never coming back. I hope your salon closes."

I don't mean it, and she knows it because we're both laughing our asses off.

But my laughter fades as I stare in the mirror.

The good news is I did wax myself because I'll never let my sister give me a Brazilian again. So I guess all the stars aligned for this one. Okay, nothing is holding me back... except all those questions still floating around in my head.

"I'll call you later, 'kay?"

"Yep. Have fun...but only the sexy, filthy, depraved kind of fun. And sneak me dick pics!"

I don't answer her, smiling as I hang up.

Dear Santa, I've even been a very good girl this year. And all I want for Christmas is Alec, Reed, Jace, and Cole...without a pregnancy or an STD. Thank you.

nine

. . .

"How am I not getting pregnant? Or getting,
like...herpes?"

I t's been thirty minutes. Thirty long damn minutes
since Reed just breezed in with his million-dollar
indecent proposal and swept me off my feet. But
now, all I can think about is how many times they've done
this.

...And when the last time someone was tested.

*...And is this just a "focus on me" thing, or will swords
cross?*

I bite my lip because the picture in my head is Jace
shoving Reed to his knees. *Damn, that's hot.* And yet, selfishly, I want to be the star of this show.

"All about me, please," I whisper as a smile blooms on
my lips again.

I need to get it together, or there won't be anyone on
their knees. More importantly, I need to man up and go out
there and ask all the damn questions. But does that make
this all less sexy?

This is why women who take lovers and smoke off-brand European cigarettes do shit like this. I'm not cool. I have a thousand questions—that I'm putting in the Notes app on my phone, like I'm making a grocery list.

Milk, eggs, lube. Because is it going in my ass? Or is this more of a *tag you're in* kind of situation? Why am I such a nerd?

My phone vibrates, so I look down at the message from my sister.

> Elle: stop overthinking. I know you are. If there isn't a dick in your mouth, then I'm disappointed in you.

I laugh, but it vibrates again.

> Elle: Dammit! Your read receipts are on. There. Is. No. Pe-nigh surrounding you.

> Me: Shut up. I'm spiraling, freaking out with too many unanswered questions.

> Elle: So ask them.

> Me: I don't want to spoil the mood.

My phone rings. I answer as my sister starts speaking right away.

"I feel like any four dudes trying to fuck you at eight in the morning aren't going to give a shit about your dumbass questions."

My eyes search the room. She has a point.

"Okay, so here's my plan. I'm just going to walk out

there like the adult I am and ask some very justified questions. Right? No big deal."

She huffs another laugh.

"Yes. Exactly. Well, hold on, there is one thing we're forgetting—"

"What?" I rush out, cutting in.

"The fact that you're saying yes to the dirtiest fantasy of all time...standing in basically nothing. Isn't that what bachelor number one told you to do? To come out in only a T-shirt? There's no way a conversation is happening. You're going to ramble and be dumb. Maybe you should back out."

Screw that.

"I'm a grown woman, Eleanor. Give me some credit. I think I can manage a conversation without dissolving into a puddle. I'm just nervous. I'll call you later."

"Mmmkay. Sure. Whatever. Good luck with that. Byeee."

I hang up, frowning.

It's fine. I got this.

I'll just put it out of my mind and treat this like any regular discussion adults have.

My sister is so off base to think I can't ignore the fact that these guys...with all their muscley frames and kissable mouths...are hot. I can keep my cool watching the way Cole likes to draw his bottom lip between his teeth. Or how Alec looks me up and down. Maybe even playing out a dirty scenario in his head.

I let out a quiet whoosh of a breath, my body starting to warm. Because I suddenly can't stop thinking about the four of them, eyes on me, looking at me like I'm about to be devoured.

Oh my god.

I shake my head, ridding myself of the thought.

"For fuck's sake."

My pussy is literally the most irresponsible monster. She's right. I'm going to need a cold shower before I—

My eyes narrow as I think, *metaphorically…to myself. I'll need a metaphorical cold shower.*

Because we all need something to dampen the sexual firestorm I feel every time I see them. I spin around, eyes locking on the closet. Yep, there's no point in fighting who I am.

If they want this body, then they'll have to play by my rules first.

I START TOWARD THE BEDROOM DOOR, THEN STOP AGAIN.

Oh, this might be the dumbest fucking thing I've ever done. I turn to face the mirror on the side wall next to the door, taking myself in as a laugh escapes.

I'm dressed head to toe in mismatched snow gear.

I put on everything I found in Alec's closet—black snow pants too long, a red puffy jacket that's already making me sweat, and snow boots too big.

Good god, even the beanie on me looks enormous.

I tug it down again over my hair, the Niners' insignia almost covered because of the way I had to fold it so that I wasn't blind.

"This is ridiculous," I say aloud before reaching down and yanking up the pants again. I do a little jump to help before tightening the belt as much as it will go again.

Oh god. I look like that kid from *A Christmas Story* who couldn't lower his arms because his mom put him in a thousand layers. The only difference is his clothes fit.

But this is exactly the cold shower we all needed. There's no way we'll think about sex…not with me looking like a jack-off Jack Frost.

I grab the door handle and take a deep breath before swinging it open and clunking through.

Game time.

Their voices echo off the walls. Laughter mixed with all the bass in those deep voices. I'm already biting my lip as I take one awkward step after another, adjusting my jacket. God, Alec wears a size three-hundred shoe compared to my size eight. I might as well be wearing clown shoes.

I bet I know what won't be clown size, though. The thought has me grinning. Because I keep thinking, what if it was? Clown size. Would it be a grower, not a shower?

Like how a clown car keeps producing person after person even though it's Tonka sized.

My deep thoughts are circulating as my stomach starts flipping over and over. Because the closer I come to the end of the hallway, the more nervous I get.

This is stupid. What am I doing?

Jace's voice cuts through the others.

"She's been hiding for a while now. This is your fault, Reed. Maybe I should check on her?"

Shit. Instinctually I try to spin around, but I go nowhere.

I'm planted, hostage to size fifteen boots. I couldn't run away even if I tried. I'd break my fucking ankle. My ass almost hits the ground, but I squat, balancing myself as my palms hit the wall, bracing my dignity and myself before I push back to standing.

"No, she'll come when she's ready," Alec levels as I mouth, *yep, and ready or not, here I come.*

No turning back now. With one more deep breath, I noisily make the last of the hidden steps before rounding the corner and coming into view. I was planning to clear my throat to gather their attention. But Jace notices me first from where he's sitting on the couch. His eyebrows raise, eyes wide as those dimples indent with his growing smile.

"Oh, wow. That's something."

Reed follows Jace's eyeline as he speaks before almost spitting out the coffee in his mouth and choking out, "What the fuck are you wearing, sunshine?"

They're all staring, and I'm regretting every bit of this harebrained idea. But I ignore the rational part of my brain and just keep going.

"Just sit down and be quiet," I rush out, waving my hand like I'm trying to swat away my humiliation.

I steel my spine and start walking toward the couch.

"I needed a cold shower, so to speak. My head gets fuzzy around all your—" I pause, looking around at them before I start walking again. "All your charm. So thirty-seven layers were my best defense."

Reed's still laughing as he sets his coffee mug down, staring at me.

I turn to Alec, who's leaning his elbow on the arm of the chair while running his thumb over his bottom lip as I say, "What? I'd say it *almost* fits. You did loan me your shirt, so I figured this would be okay too."

I can't help myself. I'm flirting. Just a little.

Alec is, too, though. Just not with words.

As I stop in front of the coffee table, his eyes shine with amusement. I glance over my shoulder. *Great, right in front of the fireplace.*

"Okay," I breathe out, looking around the room. "Obviously, there's been a change of plans. So everyone, have a seat on the couch, and we'll get started. Quickly, before I die of embarrassment and/or heat in this getup."

"Started for what? Snowboarding lessons?" Jace teases, spanning his arms across the back of the couch and kicking his legs out as I roll my eyes playfully.

Reed cocks his head, a glint in his eyes. "No lesson needed, pal. I was snowboarded once in college."

Jesus. Christ. My eyes bulge out of my head.

Somehow, I. Of all people. Know what that means. My head swings between him and Jace as my words come tumbling out.

"What? No. I'm not doing that to you—" I shift around, looking between them again. "That's not what I meant." I'm chuckling, waving up and down in my outfit. "This was to help me think...not to infer...because I have questions. Just questions. I'm not snowboarding anyone."

Jesus, my cheeks are so red. And Reed's enjoying every moment. *Asshole.*

"Ignore Reed," Alec offers before standing and making his way to the couch. "His specialty is having a one-track mind. As you've come to witness. We're happy to answer anything you'd like to know, gorgeous. Don't worry.

Nobody thinks you want to snort blow off any of our dicks."

I squeeze my eyes closed for the briefest moment as the embarrassment rolls over me again. *Fucking Reed.*

Alec sits next to Jace, but Reed keeps standing, still smirking at me. I hate him, but I also like that way too much to keep a clear mind.

This conversation is going to be harder than I thought.

Especially if they all keep flirting like this.

Come on, snowsuit of armor, help a horny girl out.

Cole stands, drawing my eyes to his. He's dressed in regular clothes. Of course, he is.

He starts toward me in his dark jeans, the olive-colored hue in his skin made brighter by his garnet sweater. Just his presence is intimidating. I swear I try to take a step back before swallowing hard, forced to hold my ground by sheer fucking will.

The room's quiet, watching with the same rapture I feel as he stops in front of me.

His eyes drop to my mouth, then tick back to my eyes. So I lick my lips, testing their softness for him, just in case he kisses me again.

My collar feels like steam's coming out. Am I hot or heated? Honestly, it's a coin toss as a trickle of sweat rolls down between my breasts.

Never mind, it's not me. It's him. The way he hovers over me, forcing my face to his as his eyes never leave mine, makes me feel dizzy.

"Nervous?" he says low and direct.

I nod.

"Want some help with him?" Cole's head softly motions toward the couch.

Who? What? I follow the direction to Reed, realizing what he means, so I nod again. Cole never leaves my face as his steady words hit with force.

"Reed, the lady said to sit. I suggest you do as she requested."

I glance over, seeing Reed slide over the arm onto the cushion while giving me a wink before I look back at Cole.

"Thank you."

My manners are rewarded by Cole lifting my hand and pressing a soft kiss to the top.

"You're welcome."

But he frowns, nabbing the zipper on my jacket, tugging it up an inch more to the top, as he adds, "Let's hope this plan works."

I don't answer because I can't help but notice that his hair looks damp. I almost lift to my tiptoes to try to sniff because I bet he smells like soap.

As if he's heard my thoughts, Cole bends down. But his hand snakes around the nape of my neck, holding me in place before he pulls me in, bringing *my ear* to *his lips.* Our bodies are so close that if I arched my back, my breasts would press against his chest.

"The floor's yours, sweetheart. But I'd make it fast because this outfit isn't helping. It's only serving to make me consider all the possibilities for what's underneath. And all the things I'd like to do to that body once you say yes."

"Okay," I breathe out before catching myself. "I mean. Yep, I'll be expedient."

He lets me go with a smirk. And I let out a breath, unconcerned that everyone would hear the exhale leaving my lungs. Cole doesn't look back as he walks to join the others on the couch. And I can't help but stare, following his movement all the way until he sits.

I'm so out of my league.

I swallow again because my mouth is suddenly dry. It'll be a miracle if I make it past question number two. Ignoring their undivided attention, I reach into my jacket pocket, pulling out my phone. Trying to gather myself before glancing at them, saying, "Sorry, I put my questions on my Notes app."

My mind doesn't want to cooperate. All I can think is that Cole intends to unwrap me. Reed wants to treat me like a toy. And I don't know what Alec and Jace want. But thinking about it has me reaching up and pulling off the beanie, tossing it to the chair.

I'm way too overheated.

"Okay," I sigh, looking up with my first question as I smooth my hair. Halted just as I say, "I just have a few—"

Because looking back are four of the most handsome men I've ever laid eyes on. They're relaxed but still intense. Each staring back with all their intentions behind each set of eyes.

Holy fuck. Standing here, even in this snowsuit, I've never felt more powerful. A smile begins to bloom again. This feeling and them...that's mine for the weekend. I've won the sexual lotto.

Another trickle of sweat runs down my body. This time it's on my back, but it still serves to keep me focused, making me bite back a laugh. I just hope I don't pass out from heat exhaustion before I make it through my list.

I open my phone and swipe before beginning.

"So let me start by saying thank you for the offer…." Poorly hidden smiles are my only view, but I keep going. "Before I can fully commit, I'll need some answers."

Oh, there are those nerves. I blow out some air as I read from my phone.

"I think we can all agree that I'm not cool…." *Fuck. Why did I write that?* I look up, scrambling my words, "I mean, I'm cool as in personality. What I meant was I'm not seasoned at this stuff like you whores."

I shut my mouth because I didn't mean to say that last part.

"Sorry," I offer, scrunching my nose, but Alec winks.

"It's fair, gorgeous. Continue."

I nod, clearing my throat. "So, like I was saying, there are things I need to know before I let you fuck me like a pack of wild animals all over this house."

Why do all the wrong things keep coming out of my mouth?

Cole adjusts himself. "Less descriptive, sweetheart. The blood's going the wrong way. And your brows are starting to sweat."

I let out a half laugh, patting my forehead. Shit, he's not wrong. Without thought, I tug the zipper he choked closed back down just an inch.

"Let me cut to the chase," I level.

"By all means, you look like you're melting," Cole adds. "And I honestly can't predict what will come out of your mouth next."

I ignore him, tugging the zipper down another inch.

Dammit, it's hot. Or maybe I'm just that nervous. *Just say it. This is do or die time, Sam. Say it.*

Before I can chicken out, I look at my phone and blurt out the exact sentence I wrote.

"How am I not getting pregnant? Or getting, like...herpes?"

ten

. . .

"I'm seeing stars."

S tunned is the wrong word to describe them. Maybe surprised is a better fit. Because stunned is what *I* feel over just casually throwing out herpes.

I'm my own worst enemy. I seem to have no control whatsoever over my thoughts-to-mouth function. The only plus about what I've said is that Reed is speechless. Shaking his head, grinning as he stares at me. *Finally.*

He wipes a hand down his cheek.

"What's a regular date with you like?"

I celebrated too soon.

My eyes briefly drop to the floor as I fill my cheeks with air before letting it out with a pop. I can feel myself blinking. That's how fucking aware I am of my awkward-ness. If I could make it stop, I would.

I'd run right for the window and throw myself out.

But I can't. Because these fucking boots are too heavy. *Jesus.*

Maybe one day I'll look back on this and be so

detached that I'll forget I was ever this uncool. Or…and this feels truer…I will cringe over this randomly for the rest of my life.

You know what, why be embarrassed? I'm about to fuck the whole room. Screw it. Lean in.

"Nobody knows," I say, looking up to add, "how I am on a date. I've never been on one. That's actually part of my next question. Is it a problem that I'm a virgin?"

All the air is sucked out of the room and replaced with panic.

Jace stands halfway before sitting back down, muttering, "Wait a minute… what?"

Reed's frozen. He hasn't even blinked. And Cole's staring at me like I'm a puzzle he hasn't figured out because he doesn't have any edge pieces.

Wow.

But Alec gives me a wink and mouths, *liar.*

I press my lips together, raising my brows at him in challenge, but he shakes his head, not buying it. *My eyes narrow. But he holds his ground and my eyes.* So I shrug before my voice is sing-songy.

"Just kidding."

A chorus of relieved sighs, grumbles, and curses accompany Cole's jaw, aggressively tensing as he spreads his legs, adjusting himself. I have a feeling my ass is going to feel the consequences of that joke.

I'm immediately fanning myself, knowing I'm blushing. But I stab my finger at each of them, making my point.

"Listen up. Especially you," I snark, stopping at Reed. "I'm nervous, and occasionally when I'm nervous, I suffer from poor delivery. But these are two very fair questions…about STDs. And since I do plan on dating after this—"

"No," they bark in unison, effectively shutting my mouth.

Jace adds, "Quit that."

My lips part, eyes traveling over them. You have got to be kidding me. I lift a hand out in front of me, thoroughly amused.

"This arrangement is only for the weekend."

"Correct," Alec answers, crossing his arms.

I stare, waiting for them to catch on. But they don't, so I press with a smirk.

"So we're pretending there's no expiration? Or that I've magically only ever been interested in a gang bang…with you?"

"Exactly," Jace agrees.

They're insane. I start laughing between my words. Why are men like this? My hip pops out as I cross my arms.

"So, just to be clear. *You've* done this before…and will again. But I've *never* had sex with any—"

"Hey, hey, hey," Reed cuts in. "Do not finish that sentence."

"Oh my god." I laugh. "But you almost had a stroke when I said I was a virgin."

"Yes," Cole levels. "And?"

"And? And I can just magically suck dick so good that your knees will buckle? And fuck like a porn star, but dirty slut is just my default? And on Monday, when we drive away, my pussy will just stay preserved like a wax statue from Madame Tussauds?"

"Yes," they answer in chorus, leaning in at the same time like a pack of animals.

I ignore their reaction because I'm too busy laughing. Hard. Like hands coming to my knees hard.

"Guys are stupid. And you guys are the most stupid."

My hair swishes over my shoulder as I stand back up. I start fanning myself again because this damn suit feels like a boiler the more I move around.

"True," Cole adds, not trying to hide his smile. "But at least we don't have herpes."

I roll my eyes.

"I was saying it as a placeholder for all things requiring ointment and/or penicillin."

"Valid"—Reed chuckles—"and yet, still funny."

Jace rests his forearms on his knees, stealing my attention because he's smiling sweetly, even with humor still behind his eyes.

"We were never laughing at you."

"Yes, we were," Reed cuts in, but Jace shakes his head.

"No. We weren't. It was unexpected. You caught us off guard. But let me answer. We're all tested and clean. We can show results to you on our phones, and nobody fucks around outside these arrangements without protection. But we're happy to wrap up if you'd prefer. Or even if you just want to because you're not on the pill."

I'm standing, still fanning myself, quietly absorbing what he's said as my weight minutely shifts back and forth. That's exactly what I was hoping they'd say. My tongue darts over my bottom lip before I nod.

"Okay. I like it. That sounds perfect." I grin, looking at Cole. "And since I'm *not* a virgin, more like a woman with a body count envied by the likes of Mortal Combat, I can also show my clean bill of health. Oh, and I'm on the pill." A tiny laugh escapes as I add, "So I guess we're raw dogging it."

I hear it the moment I say it. Reed groans, narrowing his eyes. "Why are you torturing us? Just say yes already. I know you're going to. I want. Gimme."

Oof. This version of Reed's charm is quite possibly the most dangerous. I pinch the jacket between my fingers, pulling it away from my chest over and over.

"How do you know I'll say yes? Maybe I won't."

Cole interjects, "Because we listened at your door."

My mouth pops open. Sneaky bastards. Why does that make me like them more? Instantly the memory of how Reed left my room makes me smile.

"Cheats," I snark.

Cole shrugs. Completely unapologetic. "I prefer Samantha enthusiasts."

My shoulders shake as I lift my phone, blowing air down toward my chest, trying to refocus. But as I start to read, *So when we're all fucking —*

Cole stops me, standing.

"I'm getting a drink for the rest of this conversation. Who else would like one?"

I scarcely get out "The sun's barely up" before hands shoot up from the others. Cole laughs, and I shiver at the bass even though I'm sweltering in the heat of this suit. He walks past me, stopping to turn his head, eyes meeting mine.

"If you expect us to remain even somewhat gentleman-like, after you've done nothing to filter that filthy mouth, then we're going to need alcohol. No matter the time. Now, I believe you promised expedience. Get to it, princess."

"Oh."

I smile, plucking the jacket away from me, feeling hot air rise.

My eyes blink slowly and not even fully before I turn back to the couch as Cole leaves for the bar.

I'm staring at the questions, feeling flustered. *He's sexy. Just fucking sexy. Damn.*

"Where was I?"

"Question number two," Alec offers, crossing his legs, looking at me as if he's slowly undressing me.

"Right, question number two." I open my eyes wider, trying to focus before I read, "When we're fucking, do you guys...do guys?"

Cole chokes on his newly made scotch. As Reed breathes out, "Now it's a party."

Goddammit. It sounded way more discreet when I wrote it. I tuck my hair behind my ears, feeling dampness on my hairline.

Am I sweating?

Jace grins. "Sammy—"

But I cut him off, embarrassed.

"Don't misunderstand. I'm totally fine with it. I was just hoping to be the star of the show. Because that's *my* personal fantasy. And since it's a weekend romp..." *Jesus, the more I say this out loud, the dumber it sounds.* "Scratch that. Just plow ahead."

Now they're all on their feet as Cole walks toward me.

"I mean...I didn't mean. Plow ahead. That sounds

weird. Asses aren't fields. Fuck. What I mean is you'll need to give me the rundown. How does this happen? Am I fucking everyone? Will you take turns? Does Jace fuck Reed while Reed fucks me? There's just a lot of choreography, and I'm not a skilled dancer...so—"

I'm surrounded. Eyes on me as I drown in so much male energy that I gasp. Oh fuck. I reach for my jacket, feeling like I'm boiling.

"How many more questions do you have on that app thing?" Cole growls.

"A few," I answer, trying to pull the zipper down some more, but it's stuck.

Cole slips my phone from my hand.

"Whoa. No. Give it back."

I try to reach around him as he hands it to Reed, but my arm is effortlessly moved.

"Answer these," Cole directs, still staring at me. "Do it now because I want to hear her say yes."

Now he's talking to me.

"Princess, I don't care what questions, stipulations, or terms you have. You can have whatever the fuck you want. Including the spotlight or my dick down Alec's throat if that ensures me inside that pussy."

Reed chuckles. "Sunshine, just say yes. No, guys aren't even our thing."

My chest is rising and falling faster and faster. My official answer is on the tip of my tongue as butterflies explode in my stomach. My lips part just as my knees feel like they're going to buckle.

Holy shit. I blink.

"I'm seeing stars."

"Not yet, you aren't," Reed counters.

Cole grips my chin between his fingers.

"Shit," he growls.

My eyelids flutter. "Ummm...I'm passing out."

"Fuck."

The air hits my body as Cole rips the jacket open and off in seconds, exposing the truth—me in that damn T-shirt from earlier.

I was always a foregone conclusion.

Albeit an unconscious one now.

One minute I'm staring into Cole's eyes, and the next, I'm lying on the floor hearing:

"Do you see what I mean? Every time she's nervous, she rambles. It's fucking adorable. Come to think of it, it probably didn't help the overheating."

Jace.

"Shut up and put the towel on the back of her neck. She won't fuck us if we kill her."

Reed.

"I can't believe I didn't notice she was wearing those fucking training pants. They're designed to insulate and make you sweat to death."

Alec.

My eyes blink open, slowly locking onto Cole's. He's all brows drawn together, staring down at me.

"Welcome back, Samantha. How about a bath?"

Oh, they're dreamy.

I slowly lift two fingers to Cole's mouth, pressing them against his lips before bringing them back to mine.

"What was that for?" he breathes out, staring intensely into my eyes as if I've put him in a trance.

My head shifts to see they're all looking at me like that. My gaze travels up past Cole to the top of the fireplace hearth. The place where I was supposed to come out and kiss Reed to seal the deal.

"Mistletoe," I say with a smile.

"Is that a yes?" Reed asks from my side.

I shake my head, looking between them again.

"It's a yes, yes, yes"—my eyes stop on Cole's—"and yes."

eleven

. . .

"How are you feeling, cutie?"

jace

She's sitting at the edge of her bed. Alec knelt in front of her taking his boots off her feet. I keep glancing up while I'm drawing her a bath, watching her watch him. It's erotic, in a way. I get why Alec is a voyeur.

There's so much more to see than meets the eye.

Because what I'm watching isn't him taking shoes off that are too big. It's Alec taking his time, running his fingers under the snow pants, before sliding the boots off her feet. Pressing gentle kisses to her covered knees before he sets one aside to do the other. The best part, though, is Samantha weaving her fingers gently through his hair as she bites that damn bottom lip.

Fuck.

I've never really...we've never done this. We fuck women and worship them sexually. But this is different.

The moment Samantha went limp in Cole's arms, we might as well have been a crew of medics.

Everyone scrambled, getting ice, a cold washcloth, and water. Cole destroyed Alec's jacket, ripping it off her as we laid her on the floor. And none of us spoke, hovering until she started waking up.

I'm sure we'd have done that in any same situation. Still, the attention to every detail of care makes what's happening right now so different.

Samantha's not just some chick that passed out in front of us.

We like her. Each of us in our own way. That much is clear.

"Did I die? Because this looks a lot like heaven," she teases, loud enough for me to hear.

"Stop talking for once and relax," Reed throws back, grinning at her scowl.

He's next to her, eyes never leaving her. Slowly dragging the cool washcloth back and forth from the nape of her neck to the small amount of collarbone showing under her shirt.

"No more snowsuits. Or Alec's T-shirts," Cole says gruffly. He frowns, pulling her hair to the side, giving more room for the cloth to run over her skin. "You'll go through my closet. Take what you want."

I'm not the only one that glances at him.

Mr. I probably get my underwear pressed is letting her rifle through his shit and take what she wants.

Yeah, we like her.

It makes sense. Sammy's like a breath of fresh air. No

filter. Audacious as all hell. Brave enough to jump right in and change the rules for herself.

I shut the water off, dipping my hand inside to ensure the perfect temperature before I stand and make my way to the doorway. She's talking as I lean a shoulder against it.

"Say what now? Is the beast going to let Belle borrow his clothes? Don't go falling for me, Cole. Because I'm more like a perverted Cinderella. I expire on Sunday at midnight, and I'm taking my shoes with me."

He's nodding, the ghost of a smirk on his face. "Noted."

"How are you feeling, cutie?" I toss out, garnering her attention.

"Sweaty." Her eyes shift to the guys doting on her before looking back at me. "And kind of hot."

I chuckle because I know what she means, but Alec stands, putting the back of his hand on her forehead.

"I'm fine," she breathes, intertwined in a laugh.

I push off the frame, stalking toward her.

"I think it's time to clean you up. Whaddya think?"

She nods as I stop in front of her. The guys are hovering but giving me room. We decided on this plan as Cole carried her to the room. *Alec and I made Reed clue him in.*

This way to heaven just makes the most sense. She still has questions, maybe even reservations. And selfishly, I'm happy it's me who gets to pave the way.

She's staring up at me, her lips barely parted as I slip my thumb inside her mouth, watching her close around it before I drag it out.

"I'd like to undress you. Would you like that?"

"Yes," she says, floating on a whisper.

My eyes are glued to hers.

"If you want me to stop, all you have to do is say so. Do you understand?" My wet thumb drags down over her chin, then her neck, goosebumps trailing behind. I trace a path all the way down to her cleavage.

"Everything we do is about pleasing you. We want to worship you, Samantha."

She's already arching toward me, eyes closing, as her head falls back. I lean down, smelling her sweet scent, running my nose across her jaw before pressing my lips to her neck. Leaving imprinted words on her skin.

"We're yours now."

twelve

. . .

"Falalala fuck me in the ass."

My body's quivering as Jace's lips snake over my skin. But nobody moves. They watch.

It's indescribable—the attention. I feel greedy and powerful. Sexy and wanted. But most of all, I feel turned the hell on.

And it's making me feel like I'm going to explode. My body's aching to be touched.

Jace lowers his hands, gathering the hem of my shirt, his deep voice vibrating off my goddamn bones.

"Lift."

Without hesitation, I gently raise my arms. But my stomach is doing flips. This feels so surreal.

His eyes never leave mine as he drags the fabric inch by inch, letting it scrape over my pebbled nipples. I suck in a breath, exposed before the shirt covers my face, leaving me blind for only a moment until I'm blinking again.

My head twists to the side to shake my hair out of my

face, but Reed reaches out, brushing the errant strands away.

"You're stunning, sunshine."

I can't help but look between them, trying to commit this moment to memory.

"Agreed." The back of Cole's knuckles run down my jaw as I lean into it.

Cole's touch is so gentle, as is the feeling of my breasts palmed before Jace teasingly pinches my nipples. It makes me shiver, partly from nerves, the other part pleasure. Truth be told, I don't even know where to focus because it already feels like too much to process.

"You're made for this, Samantha."

I whimper, feeling hands stroking my body just as Alec's eyes find mine.

He's taken a step back to watch. Slowly rubbing himself over the front of his sweatpants, making his hardening cock take shape through the fabric.

Damn.

The way he's staring, devouring the scene in front of him. It makes me feel heady with desire. It makes me want to put on a show. Make him hot watching the ways they destroy my body.

This is amazing.

He tilts his head, lips parting as his eyes peruse my bare breasts. I'm staring at Alec as I lift my hands to Jace's shirt, beginning to bunch it on the verge of saying, "I want everyone naked."

But Jace grabs my wrists, holding me in place, smirking.

I look up at him, confused but not speaking. But it's Reed's voice that goes first.

"Make room for me, J."

Huh? Jace tightens his hand around my wrists, lifting my arms just as Reed leans down, taking my nipple in his mouth, sucking the tender pebbled flesh.

"Oh my god," I gasp, stomach caving in.

Reed pulls away, letting me go with a pop as he stands up, licking his lips.

"Thanks for the assist."

Jace nods, lowering my arms again but not before kissing my hand. Jesus, I don't even know what's happening anymore. But call me Oliver Twist because *please sir, can I have some more.*

"Stand up, baby," Jace croons.

Can I? My legs are already untrustworthy. I can feel my chest rising and falling too fast as I stand on wobbly limbs.

These guys are making my head spin.

Not in the pass-out way, but more like I can feel their desire. I'm surrounded by it. Engulfed. And I can't take it all in fast enough. Or think about what to do myself.

Except, somebody give another assist because I definitely want that again.

My eyes close, trying to unscramble my thoughts as I draw my bottom lip between my teeth, letting it drag out slowly before my eyes open and I whisper, "Are we going to...you know...now?"

"Shh," Jace shushes. "Let's focus on getting you out of those pants."

I bite my lip again. Reed's already undoing the buckle, making my waist jut forward as he loosens them.

"You okay?" Jace whispers, and I nod because words feel like too much to even say.

I'm shimmied out of the pants as they're tugged to my ankles. Jesus, my heart's racing. I take a slow breath standing in front of them, my body on display, stripped bare and being ravaged by hungry eyes.

Whoa.

I swallow.

There was a time in my life when standing naked in front of my bosses would've been a silly nightmare. And then there's now—*Dear body, please don't have a heart attack when my dreams are about to come true.*

My lips part as I start to say something. What, I have no idea, so I close them again.

Cole turns my face to his, cradling it, running his thumb over my lip. He's staring down at me, unwavering, and all the edges begin to blur. And it all hits me.

My body is about to be the center of their universe. I'm about to have sex with four guys.

Oh my god. Falalala fuck me in the ass.

A smile starts to peek out from my lips but Cole says nothing as he stares down at me.

He's so intense, as if he's cataloguing all the ways he'll defile me. My tongue darts out, licking my dry lips. Jesus, how does he make just a look so fucking hot?

I swear this whole room is feeding off his energy, off the buzz of taunting our sexual restraint. It's like waiting for a dam to break.

Except I'm already a gusher.

Cole leans down slowly, taking my lips with a soft, chaste kiss, making me melt.

"Soon," he whispers.

Wait, what? Dams are supposed to be breaking. Soon... uh-uh, now.

My eyes flutter open because Cole's hand draws away before his mouth goes too.

"Come on, baby," Jace whispers, drawing my eyes.

The guys step back, Alec and Reed watching me intently. Jace is still holding my hand as he motions with his head for me to follow him. I lift one foot at a time from my pooled pants, keeping my hand in his, before walking next to Jace towards the bathroom.

My mind's racing, wondering what's coming. What did "soon" mean? Wait, are they going to bathe me? Is that like, standard practice? I kind of thought that would happen after.

I almost glance over my shoulder to ask as we stop at the doorway. Because there's so much I still want to say, to ask, but I can't.

It's like I'm on a sexy sensory overload.

My mind's diving into every dirty possibility while still trying to process each touch and every filthy word. And my body's tingling, aching, bursting with need but my mind is a jumble.

Until a soft touch runs down the slope of my back over my ass, making me suck in a breath.

"Gorgeous," Alec breathes.

Jace smirks at me. Probably because he sees I'm blushing.

"Come on, Sammy. It's time to get you nice and clean," he teases.

My eyes grow wide as I cross the threshold. *I was right.*

Jace reaches for the door, adding, "Don't worry. They'll be waiting."

But I blink, glancing over my shoulder, confused as the door closes quietly, leaving the others on the wrong side.

"Umm…are they…waiting in line?"

Jace gently tugs my hand, chuckling as he leads me to the bath.

"No, cutie. We're just gonna talk first. Me and you. Go over the rest of that list."

Oh. Right. Totally. That makes sense. There are still unanswered questions. I'm equal parts disappointed and relieved.

Just like when I was in high school and thought the song "Pony" by Ginuwine was about riding horses. It's not, which was sad, because I love horses. Although thank god, because the way I would sweat when that song came on the radio made me think I was going to need therapy. A lot of it.

Only the soft sounds of footsteps and a drip from the faucet echoes off the walls as Jace stops us next to the tub, smiling gently at me.

"I know this is a lot. And I know you still have questions and maybe questions on top of questions. It's all over your face. So we're gonna soak." He lifts my hand, kissing my fingertips, and I feel my shoulders relax. "We'll let our fingers get all pruney until you're comfortable and back to rambly Samantha. Take a deep breath because I've got you. In every way, cutie."

The side of my lips tilt. Because Jace has managed to master the art of sweet and spicy.

I mean, I'm standing here in my birthday suit, and yet

I've never wanted to hug someone more. But after that hug, I'd like to drop to my knees and deep throat his *dee-yuck.*

Sweet yet spicy.

Instead of doing or saying that, I take that deep breath and peer over into the tub. I saw he was drawing this bath earlier. But never realized he was making it fancy for me.

"The water's pink."

He grins. "Whaddaya got against pink?"

I shake my head, still smiling, mouthing *nothing* as I bat my lashes. He's helping me get in, and I don't know why but suddenly I feel shy. Or maybe now I just realize I've been feeling that way. But not shy to show my body, more like all of this feels so intimate. More than just kinky sex. They're kind of romantic and kind of swoony.

"You guys are literally ruining women for everyone else. You know that, don't you?"

I gasp, feeling the warm water. It's just hot enough to make my skin prickle.

"Too hot?" he breathes out, halting me.

But I shake my head again, lowering down. "Too hot? That's not a thing."

He chuckles, approving of my joke. My hands drift through the water as I lie back, knees peeking out from the top.

He'd said *we'd soak.* But Jace is just standing there, a grin on his face, admiring the view. So I say, "You're not coming in?"

Jace reaches behind himself, dragging his shirt over his head, and tosses it aside.

Oh, he's fucking delicious. I've thought about those

tattoos since the day he showed them off, all the intricate designs highlighting the contours of his muscles.

Jace is a fucking work of art. But my favorite part, besides the obvious, are those piercings.

My chin lifts.

"Did that hurt?"

His eyes glance down to the steel bars punctured through his nipples.

"Yes"—he winks—"but you can kiss it better."

My lips fold under my teeth, and I look up through my lashes as Jace hooks his thumbs inside his sweats and yanks them down. *Holy shit.* His cock is on glorious display.

Before my brain can communicate properly with my mouth, I say, "Wow."

Out. Fucking. Loud.

I squeal and immediately sink under the water because who says that? Except I'm hauled back up, laughing as I spit water when my face breaches the surface.

Jace's eyes twinkle, looking back at me.

"Wow, huh? I'm happy you're impressed."

I shrug, wiping my hands over my face, my lips barely above water.

"Well, I'm a virgin, remember? No real comparison. You could be small to average size for all I know."

He splashes me with water, making me laugh again.

"Scoot, liar."

I push myself back, feet pressing against the bottom of the tub as Jace's body sinks down, making the water spill over the edges.

"Oh no. We should let some out. It's too full."

His eyes drift down to the tops of my breasts.

"There's no such thing as too full."

I blink, suddenly unaware of how to breathe because Jace isn't talking about the tub. We sit, me staring back at him over cloudy pink water as he swipes wetness over his chest.

How is this a reality? And how did he know this was exactly the breath I needed to take?

"Hey," I whisper.

He nods.

"Thank you...for taking this slow."

He licks his lips, leaning forward, tucking his hands under my arms, sliding me closer.

Another shriek, then laughter pulls from my chest as I'm held, almost straddling him. Our legs are entwined, mine draped over, his hairs tickling me.

"You're welcome," he says, hands lazily stroking my back. "Now spill all those thoughts. What can I kiss and make better?"

I narrow my eyes playfully because I could say a ton of dirty responses. But I know he's just asking to soothe my worries. So I take a deep breath before I speak, looking down at the wings imprinted along his throat, tracing my wet finger over them.

"I guess I just don't know how it all works. I mean, I know how sex works." I chuckle softly. "But I'm obviously a newbie at"—I peek at him, grinning as I add—"*multitasking.* I don't know what the rules are. What's my role? Will you take turns?"

Damn, this suddenly feels dirty. This is when my thought-to-mouth malfunction would be handy to have around. I've never been shy about sex. But we're so intimate right now, it's making me short-circuit.

I focus on the art as he answers, but I know he's staring at me.

"Sometimes we take turns. Sometimes not. What would you like us to do?"

My finger pauses. I search his arm, thinking, because I've always envisioned being devoured, but what does that really mean? I bite my lip, knowing.

"I'd...ummm—like the *sometimes not*."

Jace leans forward, his fingers swiping wet hair across my forehead.

"You'd like to take two people at once. That's what you mean. How about having someone in your mouth too?"

I audibly exhale, nodding. Jesus. My hips rock forward involuntarily just thinking about it. He smiles, running a hand down my back, cupping my ass.

"Practice using words, Sammy." Jace pulls me closer between his legs. "They're important, baby. We need to know when it's too much or not enough. We want your pleasure, remember?"

I swallow before whispering, "Yes."

"Yes, what?"

"Yes, I'd like to be fucked by everyone, all at once."

Jace closes his eyes for the briefest of moments before hauling me onto his lap.

Oh my god. He's hard.

His arms wrap around me tightly as our mouths hover but don't connect. His breath is warm against my skin, our noses brushing.

"Tell me more," he whispers before dipping his head

and gently dragging his lips over my neck. "Ask me everything."

My arms are resting over his shoulders, breasts pressed against his hard pecs as we explore each other's bodies. My elbows bend, fingers weaving through his tousled black hair.

"I'm worried I won't know what to do. I don't want to be bad at this."

He growls into my skin, and my head tips back, giving him room to lick over my throat as he speaks.

"Just give yourself over and trust us. That's all you have to do, baby. That and be the dirty minx I know you are."

His wet hands come to the nape of my neck, curling against my skin, pulling my hair with them. My head falls back, so I'm looking him in the eyes.

"Can you do that, Samantha? Can you let us have you the way you want?"

He's right. I know what I want, and now I get to have it.

"Yes," I exhale, arching my back to be closer to him.

Jace tightens his grip on my hair, staring at me with a smirk.

"Prove it. Tell me how you like to be touched."

I lick my lips. "What are my choices?"

Fuck. The look on his face is so seductive. It's the way he stares intensely into mine with all his intentions pouring out of him. They say eyes are the windows to the soul. I think Jace's soul wants to fuck mine. I grin. He's a soulfucker.

"Well, there are all kinds of touches. Like soft ones."

His fingers from his free hand trail over my back softly. "Do you like that?"

"Yes," I rasp, but he keeps speaking.

"And then there are touches meant for teasing."

Jace lets go of my hair, dipping his hands in the water before bringing them to my arms. Water beads, rolling droplet over droplet as he traces a path up my arms, tickling over my collarbone and down my breasts.

I swallow, breath hollow as he runs circles over my nipples.

"I like to tease," he breathes out. "I love to make this part last before we take you to heaven. Do you want to be teased?"

I nod, but he raises his brows. Because Jace already knows the answer, he's just teaching me to say it.

"Yes," I rush out, almost panting, "I want to be teased."

He smiles, dipping his hands under the water and caressing my thighs. And my eyes almost roll into the back of my head. The sensation is heady. The constant rhythm of his hands, rubbing and kneading my thighs, makes my pelvis tilt forward, asking for more. For him to move closer.

"Jace," I pant. "I want you to touch me. Please."

But he says nothing. His thumbs brush up and down my skin as his hands move agonizingly slow toward my center. I grip his shoulders, writhing in small undulations over his hard cock as he pours his words over me like hot molten lava.

"I want your body to quiver, Samantha. To beg for the feel of our hands." He leans in, kissing me, pulling my bottom lip between his and sucking before he draws back.

"I want your pussy to soak my hands even in this water because you're fucking spun." His tongue glides inside my mouth, circling my own before I'm left cold again. "I want to take my sweet time until you can't take anymore."

I gasp, eyes closed, as his finger runs straight through the seam of my pussy, parting the dark curly hair.

"Oh god. Yes."

His touch is so soft, barely tracing the mound of my clit that I lift, trying to get more friction. *Holy shit.* He glides through my lips again, this time with two fingers, spreading me open to the warm water.

My body shudders.

"Fuck," I moan, trying to open my legs wider, hitting the porcelain tub instead.

Jace closes a hand around my throat, pushing me back so I'm leaning away as his palm runs up my stomach and back down.

"Do you trust me?"

"Yes," I whisper.

"Then ask for what you want."

My mouth falls open, fingernails digging into his skin as husky wanton words spill out of my mouth.

"I want you, Jace. I want you to go down on me while Alec watches."

thirteen

· · ·

"There's my dirty slut. Daddy's here."

Water splashes, hitting the tiles, sloshing and spilling everywhere as he stands, bringing me with him. My legs wrap around his waist as our mouths crash against each other.

We're embroiled in passion, licking and teasing. Letting our tongues explore each other's mouths. I'm clinging to him as soft mewls draw from my throat while he steps out of the tub effortlessly.

Fuck, my body's on fire.

Jace hoists me up, making me squeal before he grips my ass tighter with one hand, wrapping the other around my waist.

Wet footsteps slap the floor as he walks toward the bathroom door, kissing me senselessly. I don't know how far we've made it into the bedroom or if we're still in the bathroom because I'm possessed.

I'm *all hands clutching his head before my palms slap down on his back as I rub our bodies together* kind of fevered.

Jace groans, "Yes, baby," into my mouth as my back hits the door.

We're wet and slippery, but I'm not scared he'll drop me even as he pins me with his body to the door to grab the handle before he opens it, moving us back with it.

"Call him."

That's all he levels as he walks through the doorway. Two simple words that act like a damn bat call for the skanky superhero inside me. I tear away from Jace's face and practically howl like Wolverine, thundering, "Alec," at the ceiling before diving back into the kiss.

Jace chuckles, gripping my hair, holding my face and swollen lips away.

"Are you ready for this, cutie?"

I smile before he launches me onto the bed.

"Oh fuck," I screech, laughing as my ass hits the mattress.

The door swings open just as Jace grabs my ankles, jerking me toward the edge. My hair's a mess, my arms thrown above my head, showing off my breasts as I smile at Alec standing in the doorway.

God, he's shirtless and every bit the fucking man I'd dreamt he'd be. The way he wears those broad shoulders as if he wants me to admire him makes me do just that. I lick my lips before dropping my eyes to that deliciously pronounced V.

A V that lies parallel to the smatter of hair leading straight down to heaven.

Alec's hand runs up his abs, fingers rippling over the deeply defined muscle.

"Hi, gorgeous," he offers, pausing before adding, "you called."

"Hi," I answer, the side of my finger coming to my mouth as I bite it.

"Tell him, baby," Jace croons.

His hands still hold my ankles hostage as he begins to spread them inch by fucking inch. I run my finger between my teeth, never breaking eye contact with Alec, flirting my ass off.

"I want you to watch Jace kiss me."

Alec's eyes are hooded, jaw slack as he moves closer, head tilted with the hint of a smirk.

"Kiss you where, gorgeous?"

Jace looks over his shoulder.

"Here."

My legs are jerked open the rest of the way. Cold air is rushing past parts that are usually hidden. I suck in a breath, arching off the bed.

Alec's voice is deep with the hunger he feels.

"Look at that beautiful pussy. Glistening for Jace's tongue." His eyes connect with mine. "Is that all you want?"

My head pops up as the words rush out.

"I want you to jerk off watching me and then cover my pussy with your cum."

Oh my god. Who am I?

"Fuck," Jace groans.

But Alec's eyes drop back to my center. "Spread your pussy open for me. I want to see it contract."

Jace slaps his hands down on my thighs, keeping me spread as he minutely lifts his chin for me to follow directions. I want to squirm, to rock my hips, but instead I trail my fingers down my body, sinking a finger between the soft hairs on my lips, parting them.

Alec licks his lips walking backward as I stay exposed, all the muscles inside of me contracting, begging for his cock. Goddamn, it feels divine. My body's squeezing on its own, throbbing with desire.

But Alec just smirks, fixing his impenetrable stare on me, fucking every inch of my body without touching me. He takes another step before sitting in the obsidian high-back leather chair facing me.

His legs spread as his posture relaxes before he reaches inside his sweatpants and pulls out his gorgeous dick.

I mean that. It is gorgeous.

Smooth and heavy in his hand, with thick veins angry under his palm as he begins to gently stroke himself. Pausing only to swipe his thumb over a shiny gleam of precum beaded on the bulging head.

Goddamn, it's still growing. Looks like Alec's a well-above-average kind of guy.

"Eat her good, Jace. Make her squirt. So I can rub my cum all over her pretty pussy."

My eyes tick back to Jace, whose tongue darts over his bottom lip as he smirks at me.

"Tag, I'm in."

My lips part, gasping for air as Jace's mouth descends on my pussy. *Holy fuck.* The teasing he loves so much is definitely over.

My head thrashes over to the side as I gasp again, feeling him suck on my clit. Jesus. My eyes connect over

Jace's back with Alec's again as I grip the comforter, watching as he brings his hand to his mouth and spits.

That's the hottest thing I've ever seen.

My attention is stolen, my body quivering as Jace runs his tongue up the inside of my pussy, passing by my needy clit. He repeats the same motion on the other side before twisting his head to pull my throbbing bud into his mouth and flick his tongue over it.

Curses fall from my mouth.

"Oh my fucking god, Jace."

I weave my fingers through his hair, propping myself up on one elbow, staring directly at Alec.

He's stroking himself up and down in long draws, watching Jace eat me like a starving man.

"You taste so fucking good," Jace hums, making me squirm before he tugs me closer, destroying me with his mouth.

I moan loudly, dropping my head back, and press myself into his face. Jesus Christ, I want to come. But something's holding me back. It's not enough. I want—

"More..." I rasp, "I want more."

Jace sucks my clit once more, letting go with a pop before he stands staring down, chest heaving. He wipes the back of his hand over his mouth like a feral animal before speaking.

"You gotta ask for what you want, baby. That's the deal."

Alec rolls his head back against the chair, pushing into his hand, as he says, "For who...ask for *who* you want, gorgeous."

My eyes volley between them. Knowing exactly what I'm going to say.

"Reed. Bring Reed next," I say with bated breath.

Jace steps back, eyes dropping to my pussy.

"Keep it warm."

Goosebumps explode over my body. My fingers immediately massage my clit as I roll my hips. He smirks in approval before stalking toward the door in all his glorious nudity.

Alec groans, pulling my focus back to him. There's no barrier now, no Jace to block his view. He has a front-row seat to my cunt.

"Play with it. Fuck yourself. Show me how you make yourself come."

I spread my legs wider, letting him watch every part of what's happening. My eyes close. And I feel like a fucking goddess listening to the wet sounds of flesh and spit squeezed in Alec's hand as he jerks harder and harder.

My breath filters out of my lungs in heavy pants as I rock into my hand, imagining what will happen next. But I don't have to wait long because my eyes pop open again as a deep, arrogant bass echoes off the walls.

"There's my dirty slut. Daddy's here."

fourteen

· · ·

"This is mine now."

I lick my lips as a laugh escapes because I can't help but feel like I'm playing a dirty video game where I get to pick my players. Each one bringing a new set of tricks.

Jace stalks toward me. The energy crackles like two live wires exposed, held too close. Because Reed's following, dragging the clothes off his body before tossing them aside.

Holy shit.

Alec's voice growls through the room.

"Turn her sideways."

Reed and Jace grip my body in opposite places, spinning me around on the bed. My head hanging off the side, I'm barely able to take a breath before Jace crawls over me, nestling between my legs. He tosses my legs over his shoulders, biting into my thigh.

"Fuck," I moan, lifting off the bed, stomach contracting.

But my head is caught, held in place with Reed's strong fingers curled around my hair.

"Let's see what that pretty mouth can do."

Reed's dick is in his hand as he turns my head away from Alec's view to face the tip of his cock. He rubs the smooth head over my lips, leaving the taste of salty precum.

"This what you were hoping for, sunshine?"

God, I want to fuck the arrogance right out of him.

"Yes," I say just above a whisper.

But in truth, I could have never dreamed how this would feel. Because I'm out of my body but in, exploding, and held hostage all at once.

Jace kisses the inside of my thigh, where his teeth marks now reside. He's teasing and nipping at the skin as Reed pushes just the tip of his cock through my folded lips before pulling back.

Reed hisses a breath, abs hardening.

"Suck him off," Alec directs roughly.

I lick my lips as Reed strokes himself in front of me, feeling Jace move closer and closer to my swollen bud. My hand searches for flesh, gripping Reed's thigh as I flatten my tongue against the base of his dick and lick upward.

"Fucking. Whore," he groans toward the ceiling before dropping his face back to mine. "I'm going to use and abuse that goddamn mouth."

"Thank you," I breathe huskily, running my tongue over my lips.

Reed brings the tip of his cock to my lips again, growling, "Open," before thrusting inside my warm, wet mouth. I want to moan, but it's eaten as Jace runs his tongue up the middle of my pussy and then blows. A rush of cold air assaults my senses, making me lift my hips, trying to get closer to his face as Reed's dick hits my throat.

"Swallow, gorgeous. That's it. Take it all," Alec says, laced with gravel as Reed bottoms out, making me gag.

I look up through my wet eyelashes, mouth stretched, with Jace between my legs as I snake my fingers into his hair, urging him closer to my center. But I don't have to because he's already licking and kissing me in all the right places.

This is everything I wanted.

Reed's holding my head, fingers woven through my hair, tugged tight within his grip as the sloppy, wet sounds of him fucking my mouth fill the room. He thrusts in slow, deep, rhythmic movements. But I'm already convulsing, moaning into his skin while trying to open my legs wider for Jace.

"You look like a fucking goddess with J between your legs and Reed in your mouth," Alec grunts, voice husky as he jerks off harder.

The build between my legs grows stronger as Jace flicks his tongue over my clit faster and faster, alternating between sucking and making a figure eight.

Jesus. Fucking. Christ.

I'm being consumed by Alec, Jace, and Reed. Fucked and used. Worshipped and revered. Reed's holding my hair so tight that it's starting to hurt. But I love it. Because each time he fills my mouth, he says filthy, degrading things.

"Oh fuck, Alec. Get up and come here. You have to see

her mouth stretched around my cock. So ready to swallow all my cum."

I hear Alec get up, but I can't see him. But something inside me wants him to see me, to watch how I suck Reed off.

"Holy shit," I moan, letting Reed's dick fall from my mouth because Jace sucks my clit hard, letting it go with a pop as he sits up.

My head shifts to where Alec's standing to the right of my eyeline, taking long, slow tugs on himself before looking to the other side at Reed doing the same. I can barely breathe. Or focus.

I'm all feeling and sensation, so turned on, I can't think straight. I just want to be sucked, fucked, and licked.

"Please," I whimper.

The three men stare silently at me, watching me writhe under their attention.

Alec reaches out, pinching my nipple, rolling it between his fingers. "So hungry for us."

I arch my back, drawing my knees up, letting them sway back and forth lazily.

Jace runs his hand down my thigh, pushing two fingers inside me, making me gasp as he fucks me slowly. My knees fall open as he speaks.

"Fuck. She's velvet."

But it's Reed who leans down, taking my mouth, kissing me. His tongue swirls where his dick just was before he pulls away and returns for a peck, then speaks his words onto my lips.

"I knew you'd be perfect for us."

I grip the sheets, feeling completely owned by Jace's

fingers, circling inside in slow, leisurely taunts, dragging out and back in to start again.

"Jesus."

"No. Jace." Reed smirks before grabbing my tit, massaging it as he stares down.

My body writhes as I look up to find Alec's eyes. But he's staring at my pussy. Biting his bottom lip, he walks to the other side of the bed, drawn in by the smell of my desire and the soft sounds of my wetness. My feet slide down the bed, thighs closing around Jace's hands as Reed brushes the head of his dick over my lips again, pulling back only when I open, trying to suck.

"No, baby. We've got better plans."

My eyes close as I rush out, "Fuck. Don't stop. Please don't stop."

Because Jace is finger-fucking me deliciously without mercy, using his thumb to rub my clit, creating the friction I'm craving. My ass squeezes, rocking my pelvis, and my hand reaches to explore Reed's body.

"Fuck me," I say, wrapped around mewls and heavy breaths.

But nobody speaks. They keep teasing me, kneading my breasts and legs as Jace pushes in over and over relentlessly.

My orgasm builds more and more, the craving climbing higher inside my body.

"That's it, baby," Jace whispers. "Give yourself to us. We're gonna fuck you so damn good."

Reed growls, running his palm right between my cleavage before leaning down and sucking on my hard nipple.

"I'm going to do filthy fucking things to your body, sunshine."

My breaths get shorter, and my body races toward the finish line. As Reed pulls away, I arch my back off the bed, enjoying the roughness of his hand dragging back over my breasts.

"Open your legs, Samantha," Alec barks. "Now."

He grips the inside of my knee to hike it up. But I'm fucking lost. Eyes closed, barely hearing voices because I'm an explosive ball of sensation, teetering on the heavenly edge of my orgasm.

Until Jace pulls his fingers out of me, and a sharp sting ignites my clit. All the air in the room is sucked into my lungs as my eyes pop open.

Cole.

Our eyes lock, his jaw tense. He's standing in front of me like a fucking god. Chiseled and deadly fucking sexual. His head tilts, those dark eyes burning right through me.

"This is mine now."

His two fingers spread me open before he spits directly on my fucking clit.

"Alec said open your legs."

I jerk them open obediently, Alec gripping my thigh as he switches places with Cole.

"Your pussy's so fucking perfect—" comes out of his mouth, strained and guttural as the men surround me.

But my eyes are fixated, locked on Alec's hard cock strangled in his hand, watching him fuck himself harder and rougher, leaning over my pussy.

"Mark her," Cole growls.

Reed leans down, taking a nipple into his mouth before

kissing up the swell of my breast to suck on my skin. Jace runs his hand up and down my leg, lifting it to bite gently into my calf. And Cole...he just smirks because he's marking me in ways they can't.

I've never felt like this. I'm falling apart and never want to be put back together.

Cole's hand slips under my ass, lifting my hips closer to Alec's cock, making me whimper and beg.

"Tell him what you want," Jace whispers, licking down my leg.

"Come on me. Come on my pussy," I pant.

"Fuck," Alec groans. "Yes, Samantha."

Warm cum covers my throbbing clit, hitting in spurts, spreading and covering my begging cunt.

My head falls back, fingers diving into his orgasm, rubbing and chasing my release. No part of me is left untouched. Lips, hands, and hard cocks rub over my flesh.

"I'm coming... Oh my god. I'm—"

My body hits a crescendo with my breath held. But two whispered words push me right over the edge, leaving me screaming, "Yes."

Good. Girl.

fifteen

. . .

"I'm pretty sure I'll get pink eye from this shit."

F lashes of last night start firing in my head as I begin to open my eyes. Dirty pictures play like a highlight reel, making my body stir.

Oh my god.

I had a five-some. I HAD A FIVE-SOME. A dirty encounter that requires a cigarette at the end. Regardless of if you smoke or not. Because I got worked over by my hot bosses in a Gomorrahesque scene where they spread me open and...

Dear lord baby Jesus, I'm sorry. Because what Alec did might be the only reason for the season right now.

I squeeze my eyes closed harder, wiggling in place.

Excuse me, ma'am, what's on your bucket list?... Oh, who me?... To be fucked by four dudes. Check. Check. Check. And motherfucking check. Who's that bitch? I'm that bitch.

I'm about to open my eyes when my skin suddenly prickles. And I swallow hard because the rest of the night hits me like a ton of bricks. *Oh god.* Of course, my traitorous body only thinks about when she came. How else would I survive and strive for more if I remembered everything?

No. Any sane person would run for the hills knowing they're literally their own worst enemy. Fuck me. Why. Whyyyyy.

I fell asleep. *I. Fucking. Fell. Asleep.*

During my own personal fantasy.

No. That part has to be a dream. My mind is rushing, trying to sort out the night...wait—The day? We fucked during the day. What time is it? How long have I been sleeping?

My eyes spring open. The room's dark. My hands lift to my chest. There's a blanket.

I lift the blanket, realizing I'm nude, just as a deep bass of a sigh jerks my head over to my left.

Reed's lying on his stomach. His sculptured back is on display.

Another deep gravelly sound, and my head jerks to the right. Cole.

Are you fucking kidding me? I fell asleep, and they put me to bed between them.

I'm already biting my lip because this is ridiculous. I let out a breath, sinking back into the pillow, staring at the ceiling, suddenly trying to hold in my laughter. These guys came in hot, all *this is mine,* and *Daddy's here,* and what did I do? I fell asleep.

Straight up narcoleptic-city the minute I came. But who can blame me?

Them? Sure.

But it was a big morning—fainting, snow boots, baths. Alec's *moment*...all over me.

Laughter almost escapes before I cover my mouth, remembering when I started falling asleep but was still awake enough to hear them.

Jesus, I'm breathing so hard I feel like I'm having a heart attack.

My hand lies dead on my lady bits after overusing every fucking muscle in my forearm as I hear someone say, "You look like sin."

I'm sure I do, lying here covered in Alec with my eyes closed and legs still spread. After what just happened, I better get an induction to the porn star hall of fame.

I can feel myself smiling. Or maybe I just think I am because my body is as heavy as my eyes. Even still, I open my mouth to speak but instead suck in a breath because a warm cloth runs between my legs, moving my hand as it wipes away my porn resume builder.

"Time to get you ready for us, baby."

I think that's Jace. As I attempt to open my eyes, my tongue darts out to lick my dry lips. But I don't actually do either.

Because, damn, lying here feels so good. I'm so satisfied right now.

Hands begin rubbing over my body, so I hum, "That feels good." Or at least I try to. Because I'm pretty sure only about half of that came out of my mouth.

I sigh, feeling the warmth between my legs again before the same feeling envelops my fingers. They're cleaning me. God, it's so relaxing.

It's not my fault. I swear my body's sinking into the mattress because it's so comfortable. And this blanket I'm lying on is so damn soft. I bet Alec looks at the thread count on his sheets and comforters.

So soft...so, so...sof...

"Sunshine?"

My body gets heavier and heavier. And I hear them speaking, but I'm more invested in staring at the underneath of my eyelids.

"Is she sleeping?"

No. I'm not sleeping. I'm resting my eyes for two seconds. That's what I want to say, but instead, I drift further away into sated bliss.

More chuckling.

"As with most women, Reed. It looks like she tired of you."

"Fuck you, Cole."

Alec's voice fills the space.

"Maybe you should have waited before unleashing the whole this is mine now *attitude."*

"Yeah, you had her rubbing herself raw," Reed chimes in.

Jace's voice is close to my face. "Agreed, now she's too worn out to play."

I feel a kiss pressed to my cheek before more chuckling occurs.

"Aww, she purrs."

"Jace, it's called snoring."

"Nah, it's too quiet. You snore, Reed. She purrs."

Silence. Then Cole's voice is the last thing I hear.

"If our girl is tired, then she sleeps."

I feel myself lifted and replaced, warmed by covers tucked over me and arms wrapped around my body.

"Sleep, princess. Because later, I'm going to turn that ass red for falling asleep on me."

My eyes find Cole again. He's on his back, the blanket draped over his waist, showing off that deep V I want to run my tongue over. His hand's resting on his hard-earned abs. Nobody gets that kind of definition without work.

He looks so peaceful, none of the ever-present serious-ness always set between his eyebrows. I can't help but think about what he did. He slapped my clit. Twice.

My eyes almost roll back into my head when I picture the moment when he spit. Fuck.

And all he had to do was say two words, and I was in outer space. Oh, man. *The things you're going to do to me when you wake up.*

His lips tip up as if he can hear my thoughts in his sleep. I can't help myself. I roll on my side, staring at his face.

This is all so weird. I'm literally lying here in my birthday suit, sandwiched between two of the hottest men I've ever met. Who am I? What is happening?

This is a whole-ass movie moment. Where upbeat pop music would play, and the camera would pan out to show the three of us in bed as I stared at Cole. Then we'd montage the rest of the weekend filled with sexy rendezvous and filthy moments. Until we had to say good-bye. Ultimately, we'd be unable to live without each other. So, in a crescendo of a scene, they'd run down a city street. Why? I don't know how movies work. But they'd be running to beat the clock because I was about to forget them. Until they'd burst through double doors and descend upon me, professing their love. But it would be too late, and we'd know it. It could never work. So they'd let me go...*with the new guy.* Where'd I meet him? Nobody knows. But his suit matches my dress. Then years later, we see each other again, and there'd be a twinkle in our eyes. Because maybe life brought us back around just at the right time.

I wonder who would play me?

I'm smiling over my thought, amused with myself, as I reach up to touch the shadow of scruff all over Cole's jaw. But I stop. I don't want to risk waking him up. It's just that he's always so exacting, with clean suit lines and a smooth face, that the unkept shave is alluring.

I slowly turn onto my back again, my knee lifting a bit as my legs squeeze together. Looks like my bladder has decided to join in on the conversation in my head. *Lovely.* Sheesh, how long was I sleeping?

Fuck, I really have to pee. I push up on my elbows to look over Reed's back at the clock, but Cole decides, at that moment, to growl, "Mine," as he shoves a hand between my thighs.

I'm frozen, eyes wide, breath held as I glance over at him.

He's still sleeping. Even though his hand squeezes my thigh, kneading, moving up closer to my hoo-ha. And it's making me panic. Because besides the fact that his arm is laying across my bladder, making me have to pee even worse...there is no way in hell I'm letting them wake up and see me like this.

I can only imagine what my hair looks like. And the last thing in my mouth was Reed's dick, so I feel like mouthwash is necessary.

Cole mumbles something, making me panic-grin harder as he cups my pussy. His arm is so heavy, and I swear someone in the cosmos is laughing at me.

Why? I mouth to the ceiling, toward the Lord.

If I piss on this man's hand, I will find a crime to

witness so I can go into the protection program. New life. New name. That's the only correct option.

"Gimme," comes from the other side as I reach for Cole's hand just as Reed's warm palm covers my breast.

Come on.

I have to press my lips together because one sound and they'll wake up. And if they open their eyes and realize I'm pussy-tit pinned, I'm getting fucked. Without question. And as appealing as it sounds, in my current state of looking like a "used-up hooker" slash being a future "golden shower giver," I need out of this bed.

Cole grips my pussy, then releases. I hold my breath, trying not to laugh or moan, feeling the fullness in my tummy. In more ways than one.

Slowly, like trying-not-to-even-breathe slow, I try to slide Cole's hand off of me, but he rubs the butt of his palm directly against my clit.

The smallest unstoppable moan escapes. For fuck's sake. My stomach tenses along with the muscles inside of me. Because...PEE.

Fuck you, dumb vagina. I need you to think big picture right now.

I mentally will the pee back up to where it came from before I wrap my fingers around his wrist and lift. He's all dead weight as I drag his fingertips back across my bare pussy, body giving a tiny shiver.

Instantly, my bladder stops pressuring me to immediately piss the bed. So I sigh in relief.

I move his hand the rest of the way before gently placing it on his own crotch.

It's only fair. If I'm stuck in this situation, I might as

well entertain myself. My head turns to Reed. He's smiling in his sleep. Like a kid with a blankie—my boob being the blankie. Even asleep, he's overtly charming.

I move his hand easily, leaving it beside me on the bed.

Okay, now how the hell am I getting out of this bed?

If I crawl over either of them, they wake up.

I'm going to have to slide. All the way down the middle of this bed and straight off.

I take a handful of the sheet I'm lying on, gripping my fingers around it as I start to scooch my ass inch by careful inch, like a caterpillar, right down the middle.

The blanket begins to cover my face, rubbing over my nose before I'm finally in the dark. Moving ever so slowly. I keep scooting down, heels digging into the bed, helping me move down by millimeters each time.

One of them grumbles something, making me freeze just as Cole rolls over on his side. And that's when I realize how far I've made it down. Because I'm slapped with his dick.

Cole's big, chubby half-mast cock is right in my face.

He presses closer, squeezing it against my cheek, the tip of it by my goddamn eye. I'm blinking like a humming-bird, trying to stay still. But he's getting harder.

I'm about to get fucked in the eye.

I hear Reed make a sound, and my heart starts beating faster. Cole rubs himself against my face again, forcing my eye to close. I'll need an eye patch after this because I'm pretty sure I'll get pink eye from this shit. Looks like slutty pirate's on deck for this year's Halloween costume.

I don't care if they wake up. I need to get off this bed and into the bathroom.

Cole moans, so I turn my head away, risking being poked in the ear as I continue to scoot. His dick drags up the back of my head as my lips get tickled by Reed's hairy legs. I blow out tiny quick breaths, trying to keep the hair out of my mouth until my feet finally find the end of the bed.

About time. Jesus.

I wiggle until the weight of my body takes me off the side like a waterfall, dropping me down with a quiet thud.

My eyes search the ground as I wipe what is most likely precum from under my eye.

Jesus fucking Christ. Who would even believe this if I told it?

I know who...

I rise up, peeking over the end of the bed, my hands gripping the top of the mattress. Both men are still sleeping peacefully. So I lower back to all fours, crawling around to Reed's side to grab my phone off the nightstand before I crawl faster all the way to the damn bathroom.

sixteen

. . .

"You're a Ho Ho Ho."

The moment the door shuts, I let out a quiet laugh in the dark as I reach up and twist the lock, letting my back rest against the wood. *Safe.*

My fingers fly over the keys, my face lit by my screen as I text my sister.

> Me: You around? Helloooo. Where are you? Answer. It's 6 p.m. I know you're awake this time.

Bubbles immediately.

> Elle: Did you get railed?

> Me: I did...ish.

> Elle: WTF does ish mean?

> Me: It means I kind of did, and kind of didn't.

Elle: Dummy, I know that. Details. Don't make me drag it out of you. I've literally been thinking about your sex life all day. And usually, I feel sorry for you, so this has been a nice change. Now spill.

She will light me up when I tell her I fell asleep. I scoot my butt away from the door with no help from my hands as I text back.

Me: Well, it was dirty. And amazing. And everything I'd hoped for...but...

I use a hand to help me stand before I make my way inside the dark room to the toilet.

Elle: But? But what? What did you do? You better not have ruined this for us.

Is she kidding?

Me: For us?

Elle: Yeah, I'm throwing my name in the ring when you're done. And don't say ewww because you had four dicks in you today.

I'm laughing quietly as I close the toilet room door. I lean down after flicking on the light as I try to text while unraveling a wad of toilet paper. But I leave it dangling in my hand before shoving it under my chin to hold it so I can type faster.

Me: Actually, zero dicks. That's the but.

Elle: What? You had zero dicks in the butt?

Me: Yes, I mean no. That's not what I meant...dammit. I didn't have any dicks anywhere. Except for my mouth. And my eye, if you count just now when I snuck out of bed.

Elle: Rollback. Someone FUCKED YOUR EYE? What is happening over there?

Me: No! Kinda. Jesus, just listen. I fell asleep earlier after some stuff happened. I basically came, then went full coma. And now I'm hiding in the bathroom. In the dark. Texting you. Almost about to piss myself from humiliation and because nature.

The phone rings almost the minute I hit send. I jump, panicking. Toilet paper goes flying as I lose my hold on the phone, bouncing it between my hands while playing "Mistletoe" by Justin Bieber.

"Jesus," I hiss, getting ahold of it and swiping it open. "What are you doing? Trying to wake up the whole house? Why are you calling me?"

I snatch the big-ass wad of toilet paper off the seat as she answers. But a beeping sound continues.

"Accept my FaceTime."

What? Oh my god.

"No. Hell no."

"Yes, bitch. Do it."

My head's shaking. She's so untrustworthy. The worst

little sister. I can't FaceTime her. I won't. There's an ulterior motive here. But I'm weak, and she knows it.

"FaceTime me," she presses.

"I'm in the dark, remember?" I lie unconvincingly because she comes back just as quick.

"Then turn on a light. Accept, or I'll keep calling."

I groan, saying, "I hate you," as I hit accept and turn the volume down.

The smile on her face is obnoxious.

"Why do you look naked?"

"Because I am," I hush back.

She snort-laughs. "Sam, if someone's fucking your eye, you could've kept your shirt on."

I scowl.

"I hate you. This isn't funny. Nobody fucked my eye. Nobody fucked me, period." I groan. "I have to pee. Talk to the ceiling for a minute."

I set the phone down on the back of the toilet facing up.

"Put some paper down," she yells, forcing me to pick the phone back up close to my face.

"Shhhh. I KNOW." I set the phone back on the toilet, adding, "Keep talking...*quietly*. I'm muting you."

She's still laughing and making fun of me as I fill the bowl with all the paper before I sit. I don't care how many doors I'm behind. They won't hear me pee. Not happening.

I sigh, shoulders sagging. Because when I say my toes curl, the ecstasy I feel letting it all go is obscene. My sister's voice interrupts my emptied bladder bliss.

"I can't believe you fell asleep. You must've been worked over. Did you at least get some foreplay? Suck a dick?" I give a thumbs-up over my head so she can see, but she keeps going. "Who was the dirtiest...Oo. Oo. Who had the biggest dick? Did you see all of them?"

She's still talking as I wipe and flush.

"I need to get my thoughts organized. This is so exciting. You're always boring. Let's start with who got a piece first?"

I unmute her as I walk out, leaving the door ajar just enough to leave a soft glow in the room. But not bright enough to give me away. Placing her on the counter, I angle the phone, so she only sees my face as I wash my hands.

"Jace did...and I'm not telling you any more details. I did the work. I get the memories."

She rolls her eyes dramatically as she makes a dick-sucking motion with her hand and cheek.

"Sounds like you didn't do much of anything but fall asleep. Were they bad?"

I almost drop the phone again, rushing out, "No! Not even a little. It was just intense, and I'd been up all morning, worried and anxious. Then I fainted from the snow-suit. And Jace took a really, like, intimate sexy bath with me. I just think I was overwhelmed and maybe a little hungover. And when Cole did...and said...I just—"

I suddenly realize I'm rambling. My eyes refocus, staring back at her all too interested face.

"Did what? Said what? How hot is he? Because your cheeks are red, sissy."

I reach for the hand towel, drying my hands before narrowing my eyes at her.

"Hot enough."

She leans closer to the camera like she's telling me a secret, whispering, "Dude, go back in the room and flip the camera. I want to see what they look like."

My face draws back, my head shaking.

"No. Nooooo, Eleanor. Absolutely. Not."

She scowls.

"Come on, Sammy. If a tree falls in the woods and nobody's there to see it, did it really happen?"

My shoulders shake.

"That's not how that saying goes, dumbass."

She shrugs, unfazed, as she pops a chip in her mouth, countering, "You know what I mean." She pulls her arms down like she's humping the air. "Show me what I'll be working with."

I snatch the phone back to my face.

"You are not fucking them. I'll kill you and bury you somewhere no one will ever find you."

She smirks. "Look who's all jealous over her weekend lovers."

I'm walking toward the bathroom door as I shrug.

"I'm not jealous, but I'm also not even done with my food before you're trying to steal it."

We both laugh quietly as I reach for the handle.

"Be quiet. Not one single fucking word. Or I'll kill the call. Swear it, Elle."

"I swear," she whispers, clapping her hands together before pretending to lock her lips.

"I can't believe I'm doing this," I whisper before quietly opening the door and peeking out.

The guys are right where I left them. My dirty sleeping beauties. I pad back into the room, glancing down at her excited face before looking over my shoulder. I should've turned off the toilet light. *Shit.*

My brows draw together as I stop in front of the bed, teeth finding the inside of my cheek. What if they get mad? I mean, it's not like she can see anything other than their chests. And it's even darker out here, even with the low light filtering out from the bathroom door.

I look down at her again.

I put my finger in front of my lips to remind her to be quiet.

The smile on my face is impossible to ignore as I flip the camera, panning up the bed to the two fucking gods asleep with a space carved out for me in the middle.

"GODDAMN," I hear my sister yell, so I hit END, dropping my hand down to my side, eyes volleying between Cole and Reed.

Neither of them moves, even though my whole body is trembling with laughter. I lift my phone and text Eleanor.

> Me: Asshole. That's all you get. Forever. Now go away because I'm going to finish what I started. And I'm doing it with flare.

> Elle: You're a Ho Ho Ho. Merry Christmas to ya filthy pussy.

seventeen

. . .

"Okay, fellas. Come and get me."

It only took me seconds after I got off the phone with my sister to devise a plan. I could wake them up and be like *time to fuck*. But who wants to do that when I can do what I'm doing now?

Making cookies while looking for Christmassy things to dress myself up in like a slutty present...for them to unwrap.

It's the least I can do, considering I fell asleep.

The smell of cookies fills the air, reminding me I have to take them out of the oven. So I walk quietly to the kitchen in the apron I grabbed earlier, swiping my oven mitt off the counter before bending down to look through the glass.

Perfection.

Chocolate snowball kisses, my favorite holiday cookie, are risen to perfection. When the guys taste these, they'll have to forgive me for nodding off during their best efforts. All I have to do is add the powdered sugar.

Plus, if I'm putting them to work, which I am, I might as well give them a treat after.

I open the oven, pull out the tray, and inhale deeply. I'm almost just like a 1950s housewife. Except my ass is hanging out the back of this apron, and I'm only feeding them after they eat me.

Carefully and quietly, I put the tray on the cooling rack because I know I'm on borrowed time. Even with whatever hangovers they had working in my favor, they'll be up soon. And it can't be before I get ready.

Untying the apron, I toss it and the oven mitt on the counter. Before I quickly make my way back to the living room, grabbing everything I've gathered for my illicit apology. I laugh to myself because this plan is ridiculous, but I've also never smiled this hard.

"Okay, ribbon, check—" I whisper, rubbing my fingers over the material. "Thank goodness Alec's got the big bucks and this is velvet or my ass might chafe."

I scoop up a few more Christmas accouterments before heading to the spare bathroom, sneaking past Jace's room, so I don't wake him up. I flick the light, close the door, and set the things on the counter. A relaxed breath leaves my body as I run my fingers through my hair, looking up at myself in the mirror. *Here goes nothing.*

Oh. My thoughts stall as I stare at my nude body in the light.

I have hickeys all over my chest and breasts. I couldn't see it all when I was first in the bathroom because I kept the lights dimmed so low to stay hidden. *But now.* My thoughts drift back to Cole's voice, hearing him say, "Mark her."

My fingers trace over the bruises before my head drops to my thigh. Jace's teeth marks stare back at me. *Fuck.* My hand covers my center, the cheeks on my face reddening.

I'm pretty sure these guys are ruining sex for me. How the hell am I supposed to be like, *bite me. No, for real.*

Can you even put that on your dating profile?

Samantha, 32. Gemini. Dog lover. Coffee addict. Loves adventure and getting treated like jerky. Bite me, and maybe I'll let you wife me up.

But probably not because I'll just want to fuck all your friends at the same time.

This weekend just has to last forever. That's the only answer.

My head shifts from side to side, looking for who had that thought. Because it wasn't me. Can't be. I know exactly what I signed up for, and it has an expiration date.

"Back to business," I whisper like I'm chastising myself.

I snatch the spool of garnet ribbon off the counter before holding one end at my rib cage, leaving a bit showing as I wrap the other around my tits. Thank god they're boring-sized, or I wouldn't have enough ribbon.

I wrap the ribbon around four or five times before I tuck it in the middle and drag it down my body and over my junk. I'm wrapping over my hips and center, again and again, fastening myself into a red ribboned G-string. Until I come to the last bit, which I drag back up my stomach and tie in a little bow with the piece I started with.

"Are you going to hold?" I say aloud, chuckling, too scared to even spread my legs for fear I might lose a lip. "How do girls wear bathing suits like this?"

I mean, good for them. But my coochie is metaphorically sucking it in to pull jeans up. I straighten the ribbon downstairs, spreading it a bit more, laughing at myself. I'm two seconds from just rewrapping my goodies when the bathroom door swings open.

Jace's sleepy face graces mine.

"Close your eyes!"

Jace turns around quickly, laughing as he does.

I squeal, turning in a full circle before grabbing a towel to hide behind. Embarrassed but also noting that my junk stayed intact. If ever I find myself out of work, I can most definitely get a side gig as a gift wrapper. If I can wrap my pussy, I can wrap grandma's slippers.

"Are you a present? Or a dream?" he whispers.

I'm grinning, still hiding behind a towel.

"Both. I'm supposed to be a surprise. To make up for—"

"For nothing," he cuts in, hand gripping the back of his neck. "It was a big day. If our girl wants sleep, she gets it. Cole technically said that first, but I still mean it."

Why is he the best? Both hes.

I smile, teasing, "Fine, then I'll just take this off and grab a T-shirt. Better to forget about my whole dirty plan."

"Whoa, whoa, whoa. Let's not get hasty." His head starts swirling over his shoulder, so I snap my fingers. That damn dimple shows before he turns away again, talking. "I'd never stand in the way of a dirty plan. But you should let me help. You know, since I'm awake. I could sprinkle tinsel on you…wrap you in lights. I'll even let you tell me where to put the balls."

He's incorrigible.

"No. Go back to your room so I can finish. You'll know when it's time to come out."

"Fine, Grinch."

Jace doesn't turn around as he walks back out and closes the door behind him. I'm left grinning. But the moment I relax, lowering the towel, I slap a hand back over my mouth to muffle the shriek ripping from my throat. Because he's tearing back in and wrapping an arm around my waist as he hauls me up. Flush to him.

He stares at me before leaning in and gently biting my finger, pulling it away from my mouth.

"You made cookies," he whispers. "I can smell 'em."

I nod slowly, my eyes on his.

"Keep it up, little elf, and I might ask Santa to keep you."

I blink twice before his lips press to mine. But only for a fleeting moment because Jace drops me back to my feet and keeps his word, leaving me alone again.

My footsteps barely make a sound as I walk around the couch toward the bookshelf housing the record player. It's a fancy one that looks vintage, but the remote next to it for the sound system gives away how current it is. Either way, it's perfect for the vibe.

I've set the scene. Curated a moment for the classiest, most tis' the season to be horny sexcapade known to man. Christmas lights are giving a warm glow against the dark outside, competing only with the fireplace, cookies are baked, sugared, and ready to be eaten—the Doughboy's and mine. There's champagne. And I'm wrapped in fucking ribbon.

This is perfect. They won't know what hit 'em.

I'm smiling as I grab the first album that looks like holiday music and place my drink on the shelf before sliding it from the sleeve. *Okay, how do I work this?* I have to press up on my tiptoes to put the record on the turntable as I search the front of the player for an ON button.

Where are you, little button? No sooner do I think it than I see it on the remote. *Sweet.*

There's soft scratching as the record begins to swirl. And my head draws up to the ceiling realizing the music is already dialed in. Perfection. Because we'd be old and gray if I had to figure it out for this plan to take action.

I grin, immediately recognizing the song "Santa Baby" by Eartha Kit.

My hips sway as I take my glass of champagne again before I dance back to the coffee table where the other drinks wait.

Oh my god, my heart is beating so fast from excitement. Earlier today, I was nervous, but that faded because my eyes are wide open. And my body is ready.

I lift the remote control for the sound system and turn up the volume. Music fills the room in concert volume as I look side to side, waiting for them to wake up.

Okay, fellas. Come and get me.

I keep smiling, shoulders doing a tiny shimmy. What the hell? There's no way they aren't waking up. I'm having a full-on Christmas rager in the living room. Plus, Jace is already awake.

God, the anticipation is killing me.

My head's still swinging as Jace walks out of his bedroom.

Oh. My. God.

Those dimples walk right into the great room accompanied by absolutely nothing. He's naked. With his dick already in his hand. And the lights glimmering off those damn nipple piercings.

I can't decide which version of him is my favorite... sweet or saucy.

My skin prickles with goosebumps, watching him saunter toward me, hunger darkening his eyes.

"You took forever, Sammy. I was starting to think you fell asleep again."

My hips keep swaying as I shrug with a grin before taking a sip of my champagne.

"Guess you'll have to be less boring this time...then you won't have to worry."

He growls, narrowing his eyes, but a sound on the other side of me catches my attention, swinging my head in that direction.

Reed's standing ten feet away, still in his birthday suit. I can't help but think of his hairy legs as I press the rim of the crystal against my bottom lip.

"'Bout time you woke up," I say loud enough for him to hear. "This is what you meant when you propositioned me, right? You said you'd unwrap me."

Reed's smirking as his eyes drag down my body. So I do a little hip shake, dancing in place, crooking my finger for him to come closer.

Jace comes up behind me, making me jump as he palms

my ass before leaning down to take a glass of champagne. My chin touches my shoulder, giving him my profile as he wraps his free arm around me, handing the glass of champagne to Reed. Who's standing in front of me now.

"Nice touch." He flicks the bow holding my outfit together before taking a sip of his drink, adding, "I want to open you first."

I'm sandwiched as they stare down at me, with those eyes and their damn grins. And all the carefully honed sex appeal.

"You have to wait until everyone is here," I answer with a husky voice. "Because this a group present. Now be a good boy and be patient."

"No."

Reed takes the remote from my hand, muting the music, before tossing it on the couch as both guys bellow "Cole" and "Alec" simultaneously. I laugh, shoving Reed's chest, but instead of moving, he catches my hand, holding it to his pec muscle, staring down.

"You should let us get you started." His head tilts before he leans down to my ear. "Remember how much you like gagging on my cock? You did so well letting me fuck your throat."

I feel my hair swept over my shoulder by Jace as he whispers in my other ear, "Think about how it would feel, baby, swallowing his cum while I licked yours."

Oh fuck. I'm soaking. Wet rushes between my legs, making me squeeze them together.

Reed ghosts his fingers down my arm, circling his fingers around my wrist before lifting it. I watch him bring my finger to his glass, dunking one inside.

"I wonder what you taste like...maybe like this champagne?"

Tiny bubbles stay scattered on my skin as he pulls it out and quickly wraps his lips around my finger, sucking as he pulls it out of his mouth. *Jesus Christ.* I shiver. He looks down at me and smirks.

"I bet there's not a single fucking part of you that isn't delicious."

I can't speak. I'm drunk on Reed as Jace's fingers weave through the strands of my hair at the nape of my neck, making me lean into his touch.

"Trust me," Jace hums against my jaw, kissing down my neck, turning me into mush. "You'd win big making that bet."

A whimper escapes my lips as my eyes close. Jace's lips feel like the kind of velvet I've wrapped myself in. God, these two are really fucking good at this whole seducing women thing.

Because I'm seduced. Done. Sooo ready.

I feel a nip on my earlobe, causing me to shiver again before Jace says, "Is this un-boring enough for you?"

Damn, that accent. It's an aphrodisiac unto itself. I grin, about to up the ante with a smart-ass remark that'll get me fucked when a familiar voice cuts in on the sexy moment.

"And here I thought Christmas was still four days away."

I bite my bottom lip as Reed and Jace step away from me. My eyes lock on Alec's.

He's smiling, standing casually with his arms crossed, shoulder leaned against the wall.

I wonder how long he's been there. Enjoying himself. Like the delicious perv he is.

The music starts to play again, but much lower, making me blink and pull myself from Alec's stare. I'd forgotten it was muted.

"You're overdressed," I flirt as I hand my drink to Reed.

Alec's wearing green plaid pajama pants, and they're hanging low on his hips. Damn, he really is a fine specimen. A model for the male physique.

But now, all I can think about is that gorgeous cock and what it did over my pussy. Something inside me pulls to Alec. *Something? Horniness. That's what. I might as well be sponsored by lube and the morning-after pill with the kind of ambition I'm possessed with.*

I look up at Reed as I press past him, leaving him and Jace to watch me walk away.

I close the distance between Alec and me as he pushes off the wall, meeting me in the middle. His head lowers as I stop in front of him.

"You looked like you were having fun. Maybe I should've stayed quiet and watched it unfold." He licks his lips. "Because I'd very much like to watch you come again."

I shake my head at Alec, reaching for the waistband of his pajama pants before looking up through my lashes at him.

No, I mouth.

He smirks.

"No, I can't watch you come? Or no, you didn't want me staying silent?"

My lips part, but I don't answer. Because I don't have to. Alec knows the answer.

"Look who likes being a little tease." Alec bends down. "But I saw you. I know what you really want."

I blink suddenly, save the smile that's blooming.

"Saw me?"

He nods slowly.

"Chicago's my hometown, gorgeous. And when you like the things I do, a place like Church is perfect for a sinner like me."

Holy forking shit. I open my mouth, then close it again. No way. That's how they knew I was fit for the task of our X-rated Christmas special. *Oh my god.* Alec saw me watch those people at the sex club. My words drift out of my lips.

"Wait a minute. So…you saw me…like while I watched them—"

He cuts in, saying, "Yes, Samantha. I saw you. Watching and wishing. Stepping back into the shadows. Putting your hand down those black pants you had on." He taps the tip of his finger on the tip of my nose. "I watched you come at the same time she did."

I grin, but I know I'm blushing. Head to damn toe. And it won't be missed because I'm wearing Christmas bondage.

"You were phenomenal. I couldn't keep my eyes off you," he breathes out softly, and my entire body warms.

I can't believe he saw me. But that means they know exactly what I want. So I slowly lick my lips before speaking.

"Well, since you know all about me, I'm counting on my mind being blown."

My fingertips brush his stomach, gliding over the contours until I stop at the cotton string tied into a bow. I keep my eyes on his, pulling it free, before sliding my hands inside and snaking them down over his hips, letting them fall to the floor.

Alec's cock's ready and waiting. Bobbing as it hardens.

"You're getting more than a good time, sweets. I'll fuck you until you can't remember your name."

Oh damn. I keep staring up at him as he steps out of his pants. Alec's muscular thighs are on display as he rubs a hand up his abs. Over that sexy fucking happy trail until he reaches his chest.

He's so sexy. Sexy in all capital letters.

I decide to meet his attitude and turn around, letting my ass brush over his dick. Knowing exactly what I'm doing. But cocktease isn't in the cards. Because Alec grabs my waist, jerking me back, making me squeal as I'm shoved over, my ass pressing into him.

I gasp. *Holy fuck.*

His large palm runs up my back, fixing between my shoulder blade as his fingers grip my hip.

"I don't always watch, Samantha. So don't start something you don't want finished."

Alec grinds his hardening cock between my cheeks, growling as he flips my hair over my shoulder, pulling it, forcing my head to look ahead at Jace and Reed.

"Because, gorgeous, they're who's waiting."

"Fuck," slips out involuntarily.

Jace and Reed are practically vibrating with intensity. Their eyes are narrowed on me like animals locked on prey. They're both hard, stroking their cocks.

They want to fuck me. Right now. And I want it too. I want them to tear me apart. To devour every part and fuck me senseless. Just not into a self-induced coma. Been there, done that.

"Cole," I whisper like a fucking plea.

I need all of them. Now.

Reed draws his bottom lip between teeth before his head tilts toward the ceiling, voice thundering, "COLE. GET THE FUCK OUT HERE."

My body ignites. Reed looks like a goddamn Viking bellowing to the sky. Alec palms my breast, bending over me, hand on my stomach as he grinds against my ass again before righting me and whispering in my ear.

"We'll give you everything you've dreamt of, gorgeous. But if it's too much—"

"It won't be," I cut in, breathless, but Alec grips my chin roughly, turning my head to the side to look at him.

"If it's too much, you look at me. Do you understand? You look at me and say stop. And it all stops."

I nod. "Yes."

I have no doubt Alec's eyes will be on me the whole damn time. I bet I won't even have to say stop before he says it for me. Alec takes my hand, passing my shoulders, before tugging me behind his back toward Reed and Jace.

Jace reaches for me, but before I can say anything, a loud pop makes my shoulders jump. The guys look over their shoulders as the energy shifts and changes. It becomes fucking feral.

Cole's standing in the opening of the hallway, holding an extra bottle of champagne, taking a swig. His entire body's on display. He's standing arrogantly with his legs spread as if he expects me to stare at his impressive cock. And call me a people pleaser because I do fucking stare.

Jesus, my whole body is tingling, watching as he takes another swig, wiping the back of his hand over his mouth.

"Come."

That's all he says. Alec releases my hand. And even though I don't look back, I can feel the guys behind me.

The energy in the room shifts, crackles, and ignites.

Where flirtation lived has been replaced with sheer lust. It's heavy in the air, thick, crawling down my throat, making my lips part to just breathe. The closer I get to Cole, the more goosebumps explode over me. His eyes connect with mine as his tongue darts out, gathering the champagne left on his bottom lip. I'm fixed on that tongue and that mouth. I want it to do the dirtiest things to me.

My chest is moving up and down fast because I'm affected by his presence.

I stop in front of him, as the side of his lips tip up.

"You made us wait. Now we get to take what we want. How we want."

All I can do is nod because—*yes, hell freaking yes*.

He lifts the bottle to his lips before ticking his eyes back to me, pulling it away.

"Let's start with a drink?"

I nod again like an idiot. He lowers the thick neck of the bottle towards my mouth, then stops, raising his brows.

"Samantha—" He's looking at me like I've done something wrong.

I blink a few times quickly. But he draws the bottle

away, looking to the floor before bringing his gorgeous face back to mine.

"On your knees."

I suck in a quiet breath before slipping my fingers into the hand he's offering me.

Holy fuck. The way my body is already begging. My clit is throbbing, screaming to be touched and my breasts are heavy, nipples crudely hard. I'm even breathy, on the freaking verge of panting.

As I lower down, my eyes drop. They stay there until I've knelt, and I'm looking straight ahead, staring at his beautifully erect cock. It's so smooth and tan, and there's a beauty mark at the base placed over the pronounced veins protruding through the stretching skin.

I want him in my mouth, hitting the back of my throat with his hand on my fucking head, making sure I take it all.

Jesus, I've fallen down the rabbit hole. And MacGyvered a damn shovel out of horniness and depravity so I can dig down further.

Two of Cole's fingers press under my chin, bringing my eyes back to his.

"Open your mouth."

His dick is so close that I glance at it again before looking back at him. Not missing his wink.

"If that's what you want, you'll have to go wider."

Flirty Cole is starting to become my favorite version. So I stare back at him for a beat before opening my mouth wider. His thumb drags carelessly over my bottom lip, dipping into my mouth over my tongue. I suck, closing my eyes before he slides his finger out.

"That mouth's for later. First, have a drink."

I open my mouth again, watching as he lifts the bottle above my head. *Oh shit.*

"Be a good girl and swallow."

He tips the bottle, letting it splash against my teeth, cascading into my mouth as it wets my lips and spills over my chin. Hoots and hollers come from behind me as I drink until I can't, turning my head and putting my hand up as Cole keeps pouring champagne over me, smirking.

"Let's get you nice and wet."

I'm laughing, drenched, turning my head from side to side, as he bends forward, dropping the bottle, hauling me right over his shoulder.

My ass is slapped before he grips a handful, thundering his words.

"Time to open our present, gentlemen."

eighteen

. . .

"Get it wet for me, sunshine."

I'm carried, laughing, slapping wet hands against Cole's back as I'm touched and rubbed from every angle.

"You're all animals," I squeal as I'm flung back over Cole's shoulder to my feet and left breathless.

Reed catches my shining eyes, his hand steadying my waist. "Sunshine, you have no idea."

But I think I'm about to find out.

I take a moment to catch my breath, looking at these beautifully flirtatious men standing in front of me. And for a second, butterflies explode in my stomach.

This is happening. Freaking finally.

Reed's standing next to Cole, with Jace and Alec on either side of me as he reaches up and plucks the bow to make me unravel.

But I don't....*unravel.*

My head drops, eyes on the bow as a full fledge smile blooms. All the champagne has glued the material to my body and to itself. I'm basically in velvet papier-mâché, like a fancy Christmas piñata waiting to be poked by their sticks. I look back at them, shrugging flirtatiously.

"Guys, I'm ruined. I guess you'll have to return me now."

Without skipping a beat, I pretend to walk away. But they descend upon me, pulling and tugging at the ribbon. I scream-laugh being turned in circles, pushed and pulled as they try tearing wet ribbon off my body. But it's just shifting, letting portions of my skin show without letting loose.

"What the fuck is this made of?" Reed grumbles, matched by Alec's groan as I'm spun again.

Their hands are everywhere—my breasts, my back, my stomach. And I can't stop laughing.

"It's tied together," I breathe. "You guys! Oh my god, it's all connected."

Cole growls, running his hand down between my legs and tugs.

"Ah," I squeak, but he ignores me, barking, "I'm going to buy the company that makes this shit and burn it down."

I'm spun around again with another laugh-shriek before Jace throws my arms above my head, bending down, saying, "Fuck this."

The sound of ripping makes me suck in a gasp.

He did not.

"That should do it," Jace exhales harshly.

He did.

My arms fall back down as he stands and locks eyes with me. His fingers brush my skin as he slowly peels a piece away, his lips tugging at the corner.

"I'm almost free," I whisper, feeling that familiar crackle.

Pieces begin to slip away from my breasts with the help of my committed elves, who are working together, exposing me inch by inch.

I lift my chin at Alec, instructing him. "That piece loops around then goes down my stomach."

He smirks, pulling the last wet velvet strip from my breasts, following direction.

Alec holds tight to the long strip of matted velvet, but nobody else makes a move to unwrap me any further. They're all frozen. Silent, as I stand under their perusing eyes, blooming under their gaze as my nipples harden.

Alec bends down, whispering, "Beautiful," before taking the pebbled bud into his mouth. I melt. But the lips suddenly joining, brushing against my neck, wake me up. *Fuck yes.*

My head drops back, a sigh drifting from my lips, welcoming the feel of Jace's mouth on my skin.

"Hey, baby," he whispers.

The feel of Alec gently circling and flicking his tongue around the sensitive bud has goosebumps peppering my skin.

"This feels so good," I murmur, diving my hand into Alec's hair.

But what I mean is *they* feel so good.

Another set of lips, Reed's, trail up the back of my neck as my hair is lifted to expose the nape of my neck.

"Mmm," I hum, closing my eyes, giving myself over to the sensation.

But the moment I do, I'm left cold. Just like that. No

hands, no lips, my nipple popping from Alec's mouth. I gasp, eyes springing open, locking directly on Cole.

He's standing in front of me, the guys surrounding me. Cole's tan skin glows golden under the soft white Christmas lights as he stares down at me. Shadows cast between the dips of his muscles, making him feel powerful and intimidating. He isn't, though. Cole's just intense. It's the way he looks at me as if I'm the only person he sees. It's overwhelming.

His jaw tenses before he lifts my hand and kisses the inside of my wrist, speaking his words into my skin.

"You're perfect under our touch."

Good god. Those words. In that sentence.

I can't explain what happens inside of me, but I don't want the feeling to ever end.

Jace tucks my hair behind my ear as I stare back into Cole's eyes. *Perfect,* Cole mouths again before he adds, "But this round goes to us, Samantha. Remember?"

I shiver with excitement as Cole reaches up, taking the leftover ribbon still in Alec's hand. He tilts his head as Reed shifts beside me. I suck in a breath, feeling the delicate connecting piece slide down my stomach as Cole's fingers brush over my skin.

My head shifts to the smirks surrounding me as their eyes dip to watch Cole unwrap me.

Cole's tongue darts over his bottom lip. And his words tumble out as if he's only speaking to himself.

"We're gonna make you apologize over and over again until you can't take it."

Holy dirty promise.

My eyes close but only for a second before I catch Reed's grin and the wink he gives.

The ribbon peels off around my hip before it's dragged between my ass cheeks, pressing our bodies closer together. It doesn't matter that it's only him touching me because I can feel the other guys. See their hands stroking over their hard cocks. I can't help the squirm, but it doesn't help that Cole's reached between my legs to pull the ribbon up over my pussy.

"Uh-uh. No moving. Be a good girl."

The command makes me sharply inhale before he runs his knuckles over my clit.

Cole pauses, eyes locked on mine again, but this time I feel other hands on me too. It's so overwhelming that I close my eyes and just let myself feel.

"Tonight, we tease and fuck you, Samantha. Tomorrow, we'll worship."

It wasn't a question. So, I don't answer as they fall into a sinful rhythm together. Fingers slowly drift up my neck as lips find my shoulders. A palm smooths over my ass as my hair is gripped gently, the hold tightening slowly.

"Fuck, she's a dream," Reed groans from behind me again.

The ribbon tickles the hood of my cunt, gently traced over the mound, making my stomach contract. I exhale, pressing my hips forward just as lips find my earlobe.

I swear I feel like I'm floating in pure bliss.

Cole's deep voice sweeps over me, peppered with just the right amount of calculation.

"You were right before, Samantha. We are animals. That means we play with our food before we eat it."

His knuckles rub over my clit again, harder this time, making me whimper as I reach out, gripping his bicep, and open my eyes.

"Would you like us to play with you?"

"Yes," I breathe, eyes nearly rolling back into my head until I feel a sting.

Oh fuck. Cole pinched my clit. I shudder, knees almost buckling. But a strong arm circles my waist, holding me up.

"Yes, what?" Cole growls.

"Manners, baby," Reed adds sexily in my ear.

But before I can speak, a hand closes around my throat.

"We like a good girl. So use your words, cutie."

I lift my chin, inviting Jace's warm palm to stay as I say, "Please...I meant yes, please. Play with me all you want. Just make it dirty."

Alec groans out his words as if he just took a hit as his insistent fingers turn my face sideways.

"There it is."

Our lips immediately meet. The kiss is rough and bearish, as if he's starved for the taste of me. Alec's tongue thrusts inside my warm mouth, dancing and teasing, stealing all my breath.

I dig my fingers into Cole's arm, mimicking the hold Jace has on me as Reed tightens his grip around me, kissing the back of my neck again.

I'm surrounded by them, feeling their bodies against mine. Everywhere I rub my body, I can feel one of them. Feel their dicks brush my skin, or the wet heads drag precum over my flesh.

Alec hums into my mouth before he draws back, sucking on my bottom lip.

"These lips are addictive."

"So are the other ones." Jace smirks, lifting my hand to his mouth, sucking on my finger.

"Don't stop kissing me," I rasp, leaning forward, feeling Reed's hands glide up and down my sides as I crash into Alec's mouth. But my throat's squeezed tighter, sending a shock down to my pussy.

I whimper, pressing my throbbing clit into Cole's hand. Alec pulls away, just enough to make my face chase his. But it's no use because I'm held in place by my throat.

Alec smirks. "Looks like someone wants your attention, gorgeous."

My head swings to Jace. He tilts his head, licking his lips before he speaks.

"You keep kissing him like you mean it, and baby, I'm gonna get jealous."

Goosebumps. *Damn.* Reed chuckles against my neck.

I can barely contain myself, circling my hips as Cole keeps rhythmically stroking his knuckles back and forth. Reed adjusts to the other side of me and sucks right where the curve of my shoulder meets my neck just as Jace growls, "Come 'ere," diving in to own my mouth.

Jace kisses my swollen lips, not holding anything back. I'm dizzy, fucking lost. My body just keeps building, needing, screaming to be fucked senseless. Jace growls inside my mouth, gripping my neck as he pulls me closer to him. It's rough and fucking sexy.

I reach for Alec, needing to feel grounded because the other three have me floating between bliss and explosion.

He takes my hand down his body, over the hard ridges, before dragging it back up.

Jesus, I'm being devoured in four different ways.

I feel the last piece of ribbon fall, leaving me completely exposed as Cole's fingers spread my wet pussy apart. I gasp into Jace's mouth. Gripping flesh, hearing Alec groan as I rock my hips forward. But Cole just keeps me open. Unmoving. Torturing me. Letting the air prick against where I'm hottest.

My head falls back onto Reed, pulling away from Jace because I'm breathless. My mind is spinning.

Jace exhales harshly. "Tell them whose mouth this is now, cutie."

"Yours," I pant, caught up and drowned in ecstasy as I stare back into his hungry eyes.

Cole's finger begins to massage my throbbing clit, stealing my attention. He's wearing the most arrogant smirk because he knows the effect he's having on me.

It's obvious because I'm gone. Half blinking as I bite my lip. Head lolling over to Alec, seeing the red marks I dug into his chest, letting my fingertips trace over them.

Reed reaches around, palming my breast roughly, pressing his cock against my ass.

"Such a naughty. Little. Bitch." I suck in air as my skin reddens into the perfect shade of harlot. "Choosing favorites means consequences."

Oh, I'm counting on it.

I reach behind me, moaning as my clit pulses, gripping Reed's neck, feeling all their preying eyes on me.

"Then punish me," I rasp. "Because I already have a

favorite. And if you want to know who it is, you'll have to fuck it out of me."

"Game on," Cole growls, his eyes darkening, making me all tingly.

Reed growls, deep and gutturally, before I'm spun around, my back to the others. "Yeah. Challenge accepted, sunshine. But I only play to win."

Before I know what's happening, Reed squats, looping his arms through my legs, and hoists me up.

"Oh my god," I shriek.

My hands are gripped to Reed's head while his mouth devours my pussy like a starving animal. I can barely catch my breath as he stands with me piggybacked to his face. *What the fuck. This is wild.* I'd laugh, but I'm too busy fucking his face.

Reed's fingers dig into my skin, holding me in place, cementing him to my cunt.

"Fuck," I moan, dropping my head back.

I can't see behind me. But I hear Jace chuckle and Alec say, "If you make her come, I'll beat your ass."

Fuck that. Make me come.

My head drops forward, palms pressed into the back of Reed's head as he eats and licks, twisting his head and sucking on my clit.

"Oh my god. Don't stop," I almost cry out because he's so fucking good at this. How is he so good at this standing up?

I should be scared to be this high off the damn ground, but all I can think about is the tightness in my stomach. And the way I want to spread my legs wider so he can lick more of me. *Fuck, this feels amazing.*

I arch my back, pressing my face into his mouth like a brazen hussy anchored by his strong arms on my spine.

"Reed," Cole thunders behind us, and I can't help but smile. Because Reed slaps my ass in answer and growls *Gimme* against my clit.

I'm panting and moaning, desperate to move my hips more. I can feel my body tightening. I've been on the edge of coming since they descended upon me, so it won't take much. My fingers grip his hair.

"Jesus. Don't stop. Please." I saturate the last part in husky sexiness.

If you don't put her the fuck down, along with a slew of curses erupts through the room.

But I raise my voice, talking over them, "Eat me. Yes. Just like that."

I feel us start moving like he's walking, but I don't care. I'm lost in the debaucherous moment.

Another soft moan breezes past my lips, but it's cut off. Abruptly. Because Reed drops me straight down onto my back on the oversized couch.

Motherfucker.

I scream his name, then laugh, my eyes wide and a smile plastered to my face as I stare up at the gorgeous nude mob of men waiting to attack me.

Reed's mouth's covered in the glistening evidence of my lust as he stands over me, chest heaving. He runs his thumb over his bottom lip, collecting what's left of me before sucking the pad.

"Spread it open, sunshine. Show them how wet you are."

The guys close in around me as I do as I'm told and

hook one over the back of the couch before spreading my legs wide. My fingers glide between the silky hairs before I open for them.

Cole's head falls back with a guttural drawn out, "Fuck." As Jace half blinks, adding, "That's a pretty pussy."

My eyes squeeze closed, letting their words reverberate off my bones as I begin circling my fingers around my clit. But when I open them, I swear it's as if someone's rung the dinner bell. Because the way I just became a full-blown meal in their eyes makes my pussy contract.

"Beautiful," Alec groans, staring at my center, stroking his cock. All the memories of him coming on me fill my body, and make my fingers move faster.

Cole slaps his palm over my ankle, gripping it, stealing my attention before dragging me down the couch cushion closer to him as he speaks.

"*They* come. On your tits. In your ass. And all over that pretty fucking mouth. But not in your pussy. That's mine. You wait for *me*. Do you understand?"

I'm nodding even before he finishes.

"Words, princess. Use them." Cole's voice is strained in unbridled lust as he lowers onto the couch, still holding my ankle.

"I wait for you," I rush out in a whisper, my excitement obvious.

Reed's arm encloses my rib cage, effortlessly scooping me up. So I kiss his cheek as I'm placed on Cole's lap, straddling him. My hands rest on Cole's defined shoulders as I look around at the others.

Oh fuck. It's like they're getting into position. The

butterflies in my stomach have lost their horny minds. I grind against Cole as Jace steps onto the couch cushion, grinning with those dimples as he walks right over the top of couch, holding his dick, before dropping down to the floor, turning to face me.

God, I love those dimples, but there's something else I love even more.

I raise up to my knees, bringing my tits to Cole's face as I lean forward and flick one of the silver bars in Jace's nipple with my tongue.

He groans, but Alec playfully pulls me back by the hair then lets go.

"J gets to watch first. And I get to play. Don't tempt him to change his mind."

Jace tips my chin to his face. "I want to see your face when they do the *sometimes not.*"

I suck in a breath remembering in the tub when he asked me about taking three people at once. I almost melt all over Cole's hard dick.

Cole licks over my breast, sucking my nipples before he pushes me back down to my straddle. Just as Reed tilts my head back, making me look up at him. *Fuck me.* He's taking my mouth.

Reed looks down the length of his sculpted body, his thumb dipping inside my mouth. His blond hair has fallen onto his forehead, messily and sexy, as his lips part, saying my favorite word from him.

"Gimme."

That word does so many things to my body, but I don't have time to think. Because Cole urges me up on my knees, and Reed forces me to bend backward. My palms press on Cole's thighs just as Reed's dick crowns my mouth.

"Get it wet for me, sunshine."

With pleasure. I smile before licking the shiny, swollen head, tasting Reed's saltiness as he presses into my mouth with all the entitlement of a god.

"Fuck, you just got so wet, princess," Cole groans, thrusting two fingers inside my pussy, pulling a whimper from my throat.

His fingers are curled, stroking the perfect spot inside me as he thrusts his fingers in before dragging them out slowly, making me exhale harshly around Reed's cock.

Cole lifts his hand to my breasts, spreading *me* over my pebbled nipples.

"Taste," is all he commands before Alec's lips close around them. I hum, moaning, lips vibrating around the cock in my mouth.

"Changed my mind. Free her up," Jace's voice fills the room.

Reed grabs the back of my neck, keeping me in the same back bend position as he pulls his dick out of my mouth. But I'm still breathless because Alec is making a meal out of my breast while Cole's fingers work their magic.

"I've got you, sunshine. But Jace needs a hand...around his cock. Be a good little whore. Yes?"

Reed's holding me with ease as he motions with his chin to Jace. So I let go of one of Cole's thighs, reaching up. Jace brings my hand to his dick, turns my palm over, and spits into it before closing it around his thick, hard length.

Fuck me. Why is that so hot?

It takes all my concentration to twist my hand down Jace's dick. I can barely focus because Reed starts fucking my mouth again.

There's too much happening. Too much literal ecstasy happening all over me.

My hips rock, ass squeezing together, feeling Cole add another finger.

"That's it." Jace exhales. "Stroke me, baby. That's so good."

I moan again, feeling Alec suck my nipple hard. *Fuck.* There isn't a part of me they aren't touching or teasing, biting or licking. Everything in my body is building, heating me from the inside. I just want more. I'm chasing it, spreading my legs wider, writhing against Cole's fingers, swallowing Reed's dick.

My hips roll of their own volition, needy, wanting, as I try to keep my hand in time. But Jace's hand closes around mine, slowing the pace as he chuckles.

"Easy, cutie. I don't want to come just yet."

I let him take over, using my hand as I focus on the climb inside of me, letting my breathless, desperate panting become our theme song.

"I told you she likes it." Reed grunts as I undulate my body. "Our filthy girl wants to get used."

Fuck yes, I do.

He tilts my neck further back, giving himself room to go deeper. "Jesus Christ. From this angle, I can watch Cole finger-fuck you." Reed pulls his dick out and wipes it over the spit gathered around my lips. "But you want his cock. Don't you?"

My tongue follows his cock over my mouth, begging

for more as my fingernails from the hand still on Cole's thigh dig into his skin.

Cole groans and pulls his fingers from my pussy just as Alec blows on my nipple, making me shiver before leaving me cold. Three of them have stopped teasing me. And stopped fucking me as they glare down, ravenous for what comes next.

My head shifts to Jace, who's jerking himself off with my hand. I can't help but stare with my mouth agape and eyes hooded, watching the smooth motion over his hard cock.

His tattoos move with the tension of his muscles as he tips his chin toward the ceiling.

"I would like to fuck you"—he looks back into my eyes —"now."

I'm nodding, listening to the slapping sounds my spit is making against Jace's cock as Reed winks down at me. "Go on, sunshine, ask us nicely."

I lick my lips, raising my ass off Cole's lap as Jace slows my hand, hissing as he pulls it off himself.

Cole takes his own cock in hand, eyes predatorily set on me as he rims my entrance. He circles it slowly, making my clit pulsate as I stare my guys down. Each and every one.

I take a deep breath, so fucking ready.

"Please—" I lean my head back, running my tongue over Reed's cock before bringing my face to each of them, whispering, "Fuck me raw."

nineteen

· · ·

"Back Door Santa."

The gasp I make is inaudible. Silenced by their ferocity. Caught deep in my throat because Alec slaps my tit just as Cole jerks me down onto his rock-hard cock.

Fuckkkk.

Everything inside shutters and contracts around him as he holds me still, mouth on my shoulder. Like a lion biting its mate.

A deep exhale leaves my body, and my eyes that I didn't even know were closed flutter open. Jesus, my limbs already feel like Jell-O, and I haven't even come yet.

Heavenly is the only way to describe how stretched I am over his huge cock. Cole tugs me forward, trying to seat himself inside further, but our bodies are flush. I get it. I want more too.

"Fuck, your pussy's tight," he growls.

"And your cock is huge," I answer back, pumping my hips forward a few times.

Jesus, it just feels so good.

There's shuffling in the background, but all I hear is *my turn* before Alec turns my face sideways, putting his foot on the couch, lining his dick up with my swollen lips.

"I should thank Reed. You're nice and broken in for me, gorgeous."

Cole's bucking up from the bottom as Alec thrusts past where my body says to stop. I almost gag but still don't pull away. Instead, I blink up through tears, trying to relax my throat and fuck Cole at the same time.

"Goddamn, that feels good. Again for me, gorgeous." Alec presses his large cock so far down my throat that I lose air before he draws out again.

"Fuck, cutie," Jace hums, suddenly behind me, stroking himself against my ass. I arch my back, jutting my backside in the air as he says, "Let me feel this."

Yes. Touch me everywhere.

I don't shy away from Jace's touch even as it begins massaging where it shouldn't. Alec pushes inside my mouth again as electric jolts tear through my body. There's no more going slow. Cole and Alec are fucking me. In matching tempo. And I'm made wild.

Because each of them is suddenly pushing inside warm places doing dirty things.

Reed's lips hit atop my breast from my other side, licking and sucking. *Holy fuck.* The feel of Jace's finger diving in and out, mixed with Reed's roughness, is enough to send me over the edge. But I keep holding back.

Because Cole said so.

Alec pushes farther down my throat, stroking my neck with his thumb as he does. The idea that he can feel himself makes me desperate for his cock, so I try to relax my throat even more.

"Swallow him back," Reed whispers, hearing my thoughts, sliding past Alec's hand to squeeze my throat. "I want to feel his cock down your throat, sunshine." He pulls my nipple into his mouth.

I do swallow, but my eyes almost roll into the back of my head as cold liquid trickles down over my asshole. I'd moan, but I've lost all my breath. Stolen by Alec's cock.

Oh my god. My heart is beating like a hummingbird's wings. I'm either going to come harder than I ever have, or I'm going to combust into ashes spontaneously.

But I'll die happy.

Alec pulls his cock out, and a rush of air is sucked back into my lungs. He stares down at me, stroking himself against my lips.

"You ready for your dreams to come true?" The way he says it sounds like a depraved threat.

I nod, completely unable to speak coherently. What are words? There is only this feeling and this moment for the rest of time.

"Then let's get our girl fucked." Reed chuckles, and my body reacts.

Cole grinds out, "Samantha," between his teeth like a warning. But I don't care as he adds, "Stop squeezing so fucking tight or I'm coming in your pretty cunt then making you wait for everyone else to finish too."

"You said I wait for you—" I rush out, not finishing my sentence, but he understands because my hips begin jack-hammering down, fucking his cock like I'm a professional cowgirl.

I don't give anyone a chance to torture me anymore. My pussy is ready. I suck Alec back inside my mouth, riding Cole with desperation.

"Oh fuck, baby," Cole bellows, meeting me with each thrust.

I'm an animal. Blowing and fucking these men as my fingers weave into Reed's hair holding him hostage while he devours my breast.

Only one person is missing. Before I can moan in protest, Alec suddenly tears from my mouth as Jace's palm presses flat against my back, forcing me forward.

I'm chest to chest with Cole. Reed vanished in front of me.

It's like I'm on a lag. I can barely keep up because I've actually been fucked senseless. Cole's moved further down on the couch, almost lying down, but I didn't notice because his dick never left me. And now he's forcing me up and down on him, rubbing my clit over the hard ridges of his stomach.

"Fuck me. Yes. Fuck me forever," I plead. Truly plead because I want it all as I come this time.

A hard slap stings my ass, ripping a squeal from my throat. Jace grips my flesh, grinding his cock between my ass cheeks before bending down and biting one.

"Fuck." I squeal again, but it's cut off as Reed turns my head to him, jerking his chin for me to open my mouth.

"I think I want another turn."

My mouth is filled, used wet lips gliding over Reed's cock. Alec slides his hands over my back, doing what he loves most...watching and letting his cock drag over my skin as Cole unmercifully fucks me from underneath.

"Jace," I breathe out, pulling away from Reed's cock, needing him.

Cole's fingers dig into my hips, stopping me from moving and making me groan, just as Reed's voice cracks the room. "Get your fucking mouth back around my cock and suck until I'm dripping down your throat."

My clit throbs, pulsing with every word. But I press my lips together in protest, looking up at Reed's smirk.

"No more playing with our toy. Give our girl what she wants," Alec directs, standing back to watch the sexual depravity with his cock in hand.

Reed jerks a nod, mouthing *little minx* as cold liquid precedes Jace pressing the tip of his cock against the tight muscles in my bottom. Jace is kneading my ass cheeks, pushing the tip in torturously slow, breaking past the tight ring, while everyone else is fevered with sexual energy dying to fuck like our lives depend on it.

My whole body begins to tense, breath caught. Fingernails dig into Cole's chest. Bliss. Euphoria. It's all that until Jace's words tumble out and set us all ablaze.

"I've been waiting to take this ass since I first saw it sashay past me. Baby, tonight, this is mine. But *you* are *ours* until we decide you're not."

My body trembles. Literally begins to shake. And like a good girl, my mouth opens wide, as they all thrust in at the same time.

Time stops among groans as they hold me in place, inside my ass, pussy, and mouth. I don't care that I can't breathe. I'm living off the pure erotic explosion that's taken over my body. Because the moment Reed draws his dick out to the tip, I scream around it.

I'm coming. Hard and violent. My whole body spasming. Curses are spewed out among them as they pump inside of me. Fucking me roughly. Taking every ounce of my pleasure and letting me milk theirs for myself.

These men own my body. And I want to be owned forever.

Jace's cock takes turns with Cole's like a piston driving in and out of me, making another orgasm simmer inside me again even though I haven't finished the first one.

How? Holy fuck. I can't take it. It's too much.

They're everywhere, all over me.

And the sensations are making me wild because the fullness inside of me is mind-blowing.

The way their dicks rub the thin barrier between them, never letting the friction end, sends me over again. I reach out for Alec beside me, knowing he's there.

"Yes, baby. Scream around my cock," Reed grunts, rutting into my mouth, fucking it.

Jace slaps my ass again. Over and over, pounding my ass.

Cole's fingers weave through the sweaty strands at the nape of my neck, bringing my ear to his lips. "Not yet. Don't you fucking come. You come with me."

I blink a few times, feeling drunk like I'm in a haze, as I let go of Alec and slip from Reed before wrapping my arms around Cole's shoulders.

I hold on to him for dear life as his palms slide up my back, hooking onto my shoulders.

I'm fucked hard. Oh god, I can feel Jace about to come. I'm almost crying out of need as Reed repositions and thrusts into my welcoming mouth faster and faster. His words tumble out connected in one big exhale.

"Yeah, yeah, yeah, baby. Suck me so good. Make me come."

My nails dig into Cole's shoulders because I can't hold it off anymore. The tension is coiled inside me, ready to explode again.

Reed grips my jaw, thundering, "Swallow for me," as warm cum fills my mouth. *Fuck me.*

He's tensed, grunting, filling my mouth before his dick drops from my lips. But I'm panting, hitting the high mark just as Jace groans, "Oh fuck. I'm coming."

His giant hands paw at my back, holding my frame in place as he bends over me, moaning, deep and heavy, as his cock pulses inside my ass.

It's everything I wanted. But I still haven't come again. I'm right there on the fucking edge.

But Cole's dark brown eyes stare into mine, holding my orgasm in a chokehold. Making me almost forget that all I want is to come, until Jace pulls out, making me gasp and blink too rapidly.

"Shh," Alec quiets me, swiping the cum Reed left on my lips back and forth over them. "Drink every fucking drop."

I feel like I'm having an out-of-body experience. But I lick my lips, never breaking from Cole's eyes. His jaw tenses and I know whatever is about to happen, Cole is going to make me come harder than I ever have.

The guys step back, I feel it, as Cole wraps his arms around me, flipping us over so I'm on my back. His dick still never leaves me.

His eyes rake over my body just before he glances at Alec.

"Wanna make her dirty?"

"With fucking pleasure." Alec smirks.

Alec comes beside me, stroking his dick above my tits as Cole grasps my thighs roughly, still fucking me, only slower, until he presses my legs wide apart.

I thought he was in all the way before, but now that he's on top, I realize there was more.

Cole's cock is huge. And it's relentlessly assaulting my G-spot. I feel my arms stretched above my head as Alec groans.

"These tits will look perfect covered in my cum."

I jut my breasts forward, arching my back, giving the invitation. Me watching him this time. Alec's eyes never leave my tits before they close, jaw tensing just before warm cum paints my chest.

That's all it takes.

I'm falling off the cliff, screaming to any god that will hear me. Coming harder than I ever have. My back drops and arches off the couch again as Alec smears his cum over my tits.

"That's it. Give it to me. I want it all," Cole grits out between his teeth like he hates me.

I don't know if I come again. All I know is I leave my body. I see fucking stars. I may even pass out. And the only thing that brings me back is Cole's roar.

"FUCK."

I'm jerking, body spasming as Cole's cock pulses inside me, filling me with his cum.

I don't know how much time has passed, only that my

breath is still shallow and that Cole is softening inside of me.

My eyes finally open, seeing Jace and Reed taking turns kissing my hand, wrist, and fingertips as they whisper sweet nothings into my skin. I turn my head to the side, where Alec is now kneeling.

This is a dream. It has to be. It's too perfect.

My fingers drag up my chest through Alec's cum before I close my mouth around them. Tasting him.

He inhales sharply, watching me lick them clean.

"You're fucking perfect," Alec whispers.

Cole is still holding my thighs, not letting me move until I look at him. He bends forward, kissing the inside of my thigh where his fingertips left marks.

The kisses are gentle. Reverent.

"You did so well, baby," he murmurs.

"You're our perfect Christmas," Reed croons, kissing the inside of my wrist again.

"Hey," Jace cuts in, giving me that dimpled smirk, laying that Boston accent on me. "Never tell them I'm your favorite. Got it, cutie?"

His strong arms slide underneath me, lifting me from the couch, away from Cole. I look into Jace's eyes and wink as I wrap my arms around him.

"Your secrets are safe with me, back door Santa."

Reed chuckles, walking past us.

"I'll get the shower started. We'll clean her up." He adds with a smirk, "And that'll give me as long as the hot water lasts to sway her vote to me."

The others follow. And Cole gives me *that look* as we stare at each other over Jace's shoulder. It's the one that promises consequences. And it makes me all tingly inside as Jace carries me back to the bedroom for another round.

I don't know what I did to deserve this Christmas miracle, but thank you, Santa Claus and your dirty little elves. It's not the kind that gives an angel its wings, but I'm already floating on a cloud.

twenty

. . .

"There are no rules once you've been gang-
banged under the mistletoe."

I don't even know what time it is, but I've been
showered, lotioned, and finally left alone to change
into pajamas.

A.K.A. Cole's T-shirt.

Not that I'm complaining.

That is, unless they want to go for round three. Because
I'm pretty sure I'm going to walk funny for a while.
Frankly, my vagina needs some rest. I can confidently say
I'd be ordering a pussy-sling off Amazon, trying to Prime
Now it to me if anyone's cock even gets near me for like
the next six to eight hours. *Mmm, maybe like three hours... an
hour and a half... boot and rally.*

I smile as I swish my hair over my shoulder and grab
the door handle before pausing and looking over at myself
in the mirror.

It's weird. I thought I'd feel different. Maybe trans-
formed or giddy in the way when you do something
wicked and don't get caught. Or perhaps even embar-

196

rassed because of what I did tonight. After all, it wasn't my typical Saturday night. But I don't feel any of that. I feel normal, as in *the most comfortable I've ever felt in my own skin* kind of way. I do still have questions, though. Because now that the sex is over, does that mean we go back to being five people stuck in a house together? Like, what do we do in the off-time between making me come?

Am I supposed to walk out and sit on someone's lap like a proper weekend *luvahh*?

Ugh. This shit needs a manual.

Page 5, paragraph 4: How to properly behave after you've attended a jizz convention.

I'm gnawing on the inside of my cheek, pondering longer than I should, but that's me. Whatever. I'll walk out there, and if they're like, *Hey, there's good ole Samantha*, then I'll do the same. But, if I go out, and they're like dirty-slut-suck-it-fuck-it, I'll bookmark the sling and get straight to business.

"Okay. Good plan," I whisper.

I chuckle at the same time I turn the handle. The moment it opens, any nerves I've started to build fade away because I can hear them laughing and talking. And there's just something about it.

I like them. In ways I never expected.

I knew Reed was charming, but his one-liners are impressive. And he makes every conversation feel like an enemies-to-lovers movie where the characters are brimming with sexual tension and ready to rip each other's clothes off.

And Jace. Jesus, Jace. He's easy on the eyes but also sweet, like a heart-eye emoji sweet, and deeply thoughtful.

The way he sat in that tub with me until I was comfortable was pretty damn incredible. Answering all the questions, patiently understanding, and freaking sexy. He's impossible not to like.

Then there's Alec and those shoulders and those eyes. For fuck's sake, he's dreamy. But most importantly, the way I feel like he always knows exactly what I need because he's *always* paying attention. Men say they listen, but Alec could teach a masterclass in understanding a woman's needs. The moment he looked me in the eyes and said, *"If it's too much, you look at me. Do you understand? You look at me and say stop. And it all stops."* I almost melted.

I bite my lip, tucking my hair behind my ears as I walk around the corner of the hallway into the great room. My eyes instantly locked on Cole's.

Him. He's the most surprising of them all. My body responds to him in a way I could've never believed it was capable of. But it's the way he's so different than I thought he was. Cole's funny and easy with a smirk while still making me spark with goosebumps while his eyes peruse the endless supply of his T-shirts I've been wearing.

I break from the connection, taking in the others because whatever they're talking about has each of them animated, speaking with their hands like guys do when they disagree. They're seated around the coffee table. Jace and Reed are on the couch with Alec and Cole in the leather armchairs. All shirtless, of course.

I can't help but chuckle because I can't even make out what's said since they're talking over each other, eyes shining with humor.

"Sunshine, you're just in time—" Reed calls, looking

back at me, clapping his hands. "Come here. Settle something."

My brows raise in question, but I don't say anything, opting to smile because it's cute how his arms reach over the back of the couch for me like he's calling dibs.

I guess I won't be playing the role of good ole Samantha. Yay for me.

I walk toward the back of the couch, eyes ticking toward the fire.

It's still raging, making the room perfectly warm, but the tree lights are dimmed so low they're barely visible, making the room darker than before. It feels cozy and cocooned.

I kind of wish I had snuggly socks and hot chocolate and one of the cookies I made earlier.

I'm playing with the hem of my shirt as I stop behind the couch, Reed's hands already on me. But my brows furrow because I suddenly notice the empty tray of snow-ball cookies sitting on the coffee table.

My stomach grumbles on cue.

"In time for what?" I snark, smacking his hand, looking down between him and Jace on the couch. "Not a cookie. You guys ate them."

As Alec hides a smile, I lift my eyes just in time to catch Cole's grin. But Jace clears his throat, stealing my attention.

"Not *all* of them," he teases, bringing the last snowball cookie toward his mouth.

Oh no, you don't.

I dart out quickly and snatch it. Only to be grabbed and hauled over the couch and onto his lap. Laughter cracks my chest as I fight to keep my cookie intact. Jace's arms wrap around my waist, tucking me into his lap before nabbing a bite of my treat from over my shoulder with a growl.

"Mine."

I stick out my tongue, but he winks, chewing happily. Before I can scold Jace, Reed plucks the rest of my cookie from my fingers and devours it in one bite.

My mouth falls open, gasping. But my eyes are lit with humor.

"Reed," I hiss, and narrow my eyes. "You're a monster. I'm starving."

"Aw, come on, sunshine. Since when don't you want me to eat your cookie?"

Well damn. His tone is low and suggestive as he licks his fingers. And I'm completely sucked into his charm. But my face grows serious.

"Technically, you ate Jace's cookie. You might want to see if it was as good for him as it seems to be for you."

Cole laughs, as does Jace, but Reed leans in and kisses me, whispering, "Stop being so funny. It's making me like you."

He leaves a dusting of powdered sugar behind before turning back to the guys and making a joke. I lick my lips, cleaning the remnants, but I'm happy he isn't looking at me. *Because I'm shy?* What is going on? I was literally on my knees, deep in cock, like an hour ago. The time for shy left the building when I asked someone to come on me.

But here I am, blushing and trying not to smile.

A thought niggles. *That kiss was sweet and not even remotely laced with intention.* Reed just kissed me because he wanted to. Like he *likes* me. Not like he wanted to fuck me.

That feels against the rules.

My eyes search the room, but everyone else seems cool and collected. They're not trying to examine the rules like a nerd. Okay. Yep. I'm overthinking. Of course, that's what I'm doing.

Page 7, paragraph 2: There are no rules once you've been gang-banged under the mistletoe.

I take a deep breath snuggling up to Jace, who's laughing.

Just go with the flow, Samantha. We're just kissing each other like we like each other. Easy peasy. It's not complicated at all.

Jace's fingers press under my chin, bringing my eyes to his.

"You good?"

I smirk.

"I'm hungry. I'm not a girl who doesn't eat. And the leftovers I snuck earlier have been fucked off me. This ass is round for a reason, and I'd like to keep it that way."

Alec chuckles, hearing what I said. "Well, in that case, you should know I saved you some cookies. But first, as Reed said, you need to vote on something. Break a tie for us. Then we'll properly feed you." He leans in, giving me a wink. "Because I very much like that ass."

I blush. I can't help it.

"Yeah," Jace whispers in my ear, discreetly bucking his hips. "It's pretty fucking memorable."

I stifle my laugh, feeling Jace's arms tighten around me as he nuzzles my neck.

"Fine. Hit me," I shoot out. "But full disclosure, my

vote goes to whatever side Alec's on...because *he* saved me cookies."

I emphasize my words, laughing as they lose all their luster because Jace tickles me as Reed grabs my hand, pretending to bite it.

Alec smiles, snapping his fingers, excited like he's going to tell me a secret, but Cole yells over him, pointing his finger at him, "Nooo, shut the fuck up. Don't you tell her what you chose. No stealing the vote, you asshole cheat."

My knees curl into Jace's lap even more as I smile ear to ear, feeling his lips brush my neck. I lean back against his chest and clap my hands like a villain.

"Oh, now I'm for sure voting for Alec. Let me guess," I rush out, looking up at Jace. "You two are on the same side."

"How'd you know?" Jace rushes out, showing off that dimple.

"Because it's good against evil—Alec and you versus Reed and Cole."

Cole groans but catches my eyes as he sits back in his chair, absentmindedly running his hand over his abs. He's staring at me, and I swear I can almost see his devious plan unfold. I'm already chuckling as he speaks.

"I should have seen this shit coming. Princess, I *will* play dirty. Because this is the most serious question I will ever ask you. And trust me when I say, if you answer correctly, I will reward you with food, but only after I *eat*."

I bat my lashes. "Well then, good thing I have no loyalties. I can absolutely be bought with dirty promises. My vote is yours."

Alec laughs, shoving his shoulder. "Now, who's stealing the vote, dick." His eyes shift to mine. "I can top his offer…" The words roll off his tongue laced with sexuality. "Baby, I'll play with your hair."

I moan, eyes rolling back as they laugh.

"Beat that," Alec throws out as Cole bellows more laughter.

I bite my lip, enjoying myself. They're so attractive. No, that's not it. They're habit-forming. Watching them verbally spar and laugh. Just listening to the shit-talk. I could sit here all night soaking them in.

There's nothing like a good bromance. And being the only girl who gets to witness it is pretty fucking intoxicating. I'll need to detox with some super boring assholes once this weekend is over, just to set me straight.

"Just ask her already." Reed chuckles, pulling my feet onto his lap.

Cole takes a deep breath, leaning in, elbows coming to his knees. The whole room grows quiet as if he's about to say the most serious thing ever said. But then a smirk graces his lips.

"*Die Hard*…Christmas movie? Yay or nay."

"Have a seat," Cole growls into my ear as his muscular arm hooks around my waist, lifting me.

I squeal as I'm plopped down onto the stool in front of the kitchen island, still grateful for the assist since my legs feel like I'm walking on Jell-O. Jesus, I've never been so happy to agree that *Die Hard* is a Christmas movie. Because getting yippee-ki-ate out spread across the coffee table is definitely the highlight of my life.

"Thank you," I breathe out.

He gives me a sly look. "It's the least I can do. Since I'm the cause of those gorgeous stems not working properly."

My tongue darts out, swiping over dry lips as he stares down at me. The smirk on his face is still doing delicious things to me. Cole leans down slowly, pressing a kiss to my cheek before I'm left, eyelashes fluttering, to watch him walk around the counter.

I adjust on the stool, bringing my hands to the cold marble counter as I watch my very own version of *Top Chef* meets *Magic Mike* unfold in front of me.

"Hold on. You're actually cooking for me?" I rasp. "I thought you didn't know how."

Not that I'm complaining. I wouldn't even know how to. I can barely string cohesive thoughts together after what just went down.

Reed smirks with a carton of eggs in hand.

"We don't cook. But we know breakfast, sunshine. We aren't complete heathens."

Lies. They are. The best fucking kind.

I blink, stifling a chuckle. My eyes shift over to Alec, who's pulling frozen waffles out of the freezer. He grins, raising his brows.

"I'm thinking syrup, chocolate sauce, and whipped cream."

I nod, immediately picturing myself as the waffle.

Jace catches a peach midair from Cole, stealing my attention. His tattooed chest is on display as it rises and falls a bit faster. And I swear, it doesn't matter that I was just handled in the most spectacular way. My body is ablaze all over again.

Our eyes stay connected as he brings the peach to his mouth, leaning in to smell it before he takes a bite.

I shiver. *Fuck.*

Jace licks the glistening juice off his lips, smiling at me as he chews before he says, "Keep looking at me like that, and I might put you through round two of the coffee table."

The room grows silent, only the sound of butter crackling in the pan. Jace walks around the island, taking another bite but stops as he comes to stand next to me.

I shift on the stool and bring my knees to either side of his defined body. But he says nothing, just lifts the peach to my lips.

"Bite?"

I nod, but I don't even get to chew it before Jace runs his tongue up my chin, collecting the spillage before diving into my mouth. Somehow my bite becomes his, stolen straight from my mouth along with all my senses. Because before I know it, that same peach is slicked over my pussy, making me gasp just before Jace disappears under the countertop, and I'm left to hold the marble for my dear life. My eyes are already rolling into the back of my head as Cole grins, throwing his words over his shoulder.

"Make her come quick, J. Eggs are up."

Jesus, if this is our Saturday night, I can't wait to see what the rest of the weekend holds.

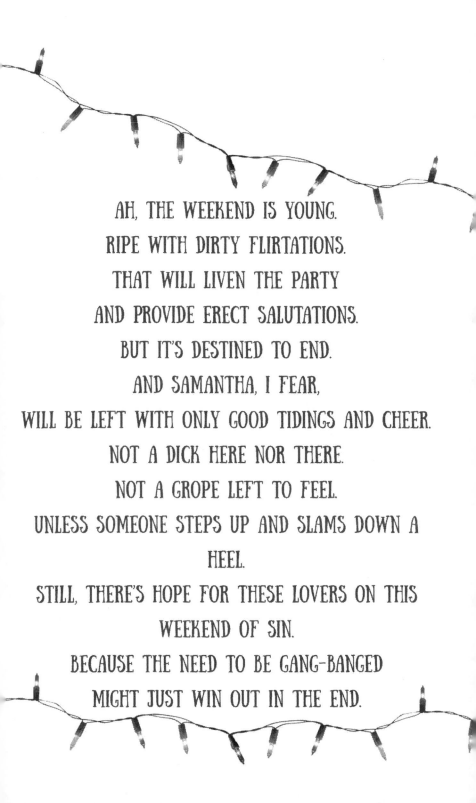

AH, THE WEEKEND IS YOUNG.

RIPE WITH DIRTY FLIRTATIONS.

THAT WILL LIVEN THE PARTY

AND PROVIDE ERECT SALUTATIONS.

BUT IT'S DESTINED TO END.

AND SAMANTHA, I FEAR,

WILL BE LEFT WITH ONLY GOOD TIDINGS AND CHEER.

NOT A DICK HERE NOR THERE.

NOT A GROPE LEFT TO FEEL.

UNLESS SOMEONE STEPS UP AND SLAMS DOWN A HEEL.

STILL, THERE'S HOPE FOR THESE LOVERS ON THIS WEEKEND OF SIN.

BECAUSE THE NEED TO BE GANG-BANGED MIGHT JUST WIN OUT IN THE END.

twenty-one

· · ·

"We're not done with you yet, princess."

"**F**ull house." I laugh because they groan.

"How the fuck are you so lucky at this game?" Cole smirks.

"We're cursed. This is bullshit." Reed tosses his cards.

I stick out my tongue as I lean forward to gather all the chips before saying, "Come to mama."

"I'm out," Alec grumbles. "I'm cutting my losses."

Laughter bursts from my chest. "There is no quitting at strip poker, silly. You're in until you're out...so to speak." I give a wink. "Now off with..." My head cranes to see what they still have on, and a smirk stretches across my face.

"You guys better hope it's warm enough in here because it's time to strip those boxer briefs."

God, this is so fun. If I was home, I'd be cleaning my house, running errands, and watching Instagram reels about the travel I'll never do, because that's what Sunday is for. But this is *way* better. Reed even put on skivvies for our game.

"What's it been, like six hands?" Jace prods, standing up. I nod, giving him a wink as his Boston accent lays thick over the word *ringah* as it's hurled at me.

I sit back in my chair, propping my feet up on the card table, with a grin, tipping the clear poker visor I found.

"Maybe…but you're still a loser, so get to it. I'm a very important and impatient woman."

There's no point in lying because I cleaned up immediately. I'd acted like I didn't know how to play when the truth is that my sister and I are basically professional card sharks. Gramps taught us well.

Reed leans forward in his chair to steal my eyes. "Sunshine. You realize once you win…I win."

I bite my bottom lip, looking up at him through my lashes.

"There's a flaw in your thinking, Reed. Once I win, *you're* nude, and *I'm* clothed." He narrows his eyes at me, but I smile sweetly as I continue. "Did you think I'd just jump out of my T-shirt the moment your dick entered the chat?"

"Yeah," he huffs with no apology for his arrogance, making me laugh.

Cole growls from across the table, his lip tipping up into a sneer.

Why is this so fun? His hands slap down on the table, making the chips clink and bounce around the felt as he pushes to stand.

"All right, princess. Name your price." He tosses a red chip at me, the one that we're pretending is worth a hundred dollars. "How much to get you out of that shirt?"

My mouth drops open, fake shock oozing off me.

"Are you trying to buy my nudity? What kind of woman do you take me for?"

His jaw tenses, a smirk hidden inside of it. Our eyes are locked, his boring into mine.

"The kind who wants me to put you over this table and make that ass red before I spread your cheeks and fuck you while you suck Reed off."

I swallow, squeezing my thighs together, feeling heat rush through my center, leaving me slick with my need.

"Umm," I say huskily, swallowing again before I purposely poke the bear. "That might've been true a week ago, but two for the money seems cheap now. Don't you think? I'm going to need a better offer."

A green chip lands in the middle of the table—those were the five-hundred-dollar chips. I shift my head to see Alec smirking.

"My buy-in. To eat that delicious pussy before they start."

I bite the tip of my tongue before drawing my bottom lip in and letting it go slowly.

"Interesting offer, but it's still light."

Reed rubs his already hardening cock, tossing a thousand-dollar chip onto the table.

"You realize that pussy is priceless. I'll spend all the fake money I have."

My head tips back as my laughter bounces off the ceiling, but it's Jace who steals the spotlight and seals the deal.

His arms spread, pushing all the chips into the center of the table.

"All of this to make Reed stand in the corner and watch us fuck you."

"Deal," I scream, then shriek as I'm hauled from my chair and thrown over Reed's shoulder.

My bare ass is slapped as I'm carried to the middle of the great room. Reed sets me to my feet, brushing my errant hair from my face.

"You want me to watch, huh? Fine, but you'll put on a show. Now be a good little slut and dance for us...but really just for me."

His big hands are engulfing the sides of my face as I stare up at him with only the hint of a grin.

"Mmmkay...but a girl needs music."

Reed's eyes don't leave mine as he says, "Alec. Our Lolita would like some mood music."

"And find something Christmassy," I add, raising to my tiptoes, melting into a body-numbing kiss from Reed.

I'm lost in the moment and the fantasy of stripping for my guys, as static sounds through the speakers, making goose-bumps explode over my arms. Because just knowing their eyes will be glued to me makes me feel like a sexual goddess.

I slowly start to pull away from Reed, hearing the first note of the music before my hips start to sway. He groans, pushing me farther away as he steps back. Eyes never leaving me. I tip my face to the ceiling letting the jazzy instrumental seep into my bones, my fingers playfully lifting the hem of my shirt, exposing the tops of my thighs.

"Take it off, baby," Alec shouts, giving me a wink as I turn toward him, biting my lip.

With a smile, I pull one side of my T-shirt up to my hip, showing off the absence of my underwear before switching to the other side as I swirl my hips.

"Fuck yeah," Jace bellows before whistling with two fingers.

I raise my arms in the air, looking over my shoulder, locking stares with Cole as he tilts his head and smirks. My hips rock back and forth as I close my eyes, relishing in the feeling of their attention.

God, it's addictive.

Hollers and cheers follow every movement as I put on the best show I know how, even dancing over to the bookcase where Alec is standing. The tip of his lips makes his handsome face irresistible. So I blow him a kiss, grabbing the corner of the bookcase to use as a pole.

I hitch my leg up, foot on one of the shelves, holding the edge with one hand as I grind against it. Giving my best 80s music video groupie rendition.

His lips gather around a silent whoosh of breath before he reaches down to adjust himself.

Who am I? Don't look me directly in the eyes because I am a sexual diva right now.

I grip the rim of the shelf tighter, throwing my head back to flip my hair around, but apparently, it's just a little too hard because the record skips. And the moment I drop down into a proper stripper squat, knees spread, ass out, all I hear is *ALVINNNN* yelled through the room.

Whiplash. I almost injure myself with the quickness of my double take. But all I see are Alec's shoulders shaking. He raises his hands, shrugging as the high-pitched Chipmunk chorus begins.

"You said Christmassy…nothing's more festive than Chipmunks."

My mouth drops open, eyes wide with humor. "Oh really?"

He's so amused that it makes me narrow my eyes as I walk backward. "I think rodents really do it for ya. I mean, I knew gerbils were a thing, but I've never heard of a cartoon Chipmunk kink."

Before he can speak, I add, "But who am I to judge. Maybe you just need a reminder of what's right in front of you. I'm no Theodore but—" I lift my shirt, flashing not just my tits, before dropping it back down with a grin.

My bravado is short-lived because Alec lunges, making me scream with laughter as I just barely escape, tripping over my feet, turning to run. My hair flies behind me as shrieks and laughter crack my chest.

The guys kick into motion and I'm narrowly missed by Reed as his arms dart out for me, sending me running toward the back door.

"No," I scream, laughing.

My feet carry me quickly. To where, I have no idea. I can't go outside, or I'll die of hypothermia. But the only thing that matters is not getting caught. So maybe I am willing to frosty the snowman myself.

Cole calls out some football call, thundering, *Alpha-kick-back-niner-something,* as he jumps the couch to cut me off, making me yelp and glance backward.

But that's my demise because just as I reach for the doorknob, I'm suddenly scooped up like a bride forced to submit as I look directly into Jace's eyes.

My arms clasp around his neck with my smile gathered from ear to ear.

"Interception." He grins.

"Unfair," I pant, my cheeks flushed. "But I can honestly say I've never been happier to lose." *Because very naughty things are about to happen.*

Alec sidles up beside Jace, leaning down to kiss my forehead.

"You're the cutest goddamn thing I've ever laid my eyes on. I mean...no Theodore, but I think I'll keep you."

I'm smiling ear to ear as my head falls back, dizzy over his words as an upside-down view of the hot tub comes into focus.

"Hey." I snap back up. "Does that work?"

Cole laughs, coming up on the other side of Jace.

"Reed already turned it on, princess."

SLICK, WET HANDS DRIFT OVER MY BODY AS I'M PASSED over to Alec's lap. I straddle him, grinding my bare pussy over his hard cock, our tongues dancing. We're locked in a heated kiss as the bubbles from the hot tub pop around us. Sounding like the crackle of our chemistry.

"Samantha," he delivers with deep bass forcing us apart, "I want to watch my cock slide inside you."

My moan drifts out as I run my wet palms up the back of his neck.

"Yes, please," I breathe out huskily.

There's no hesitation as Alec lifts me from the water and turns us around, placing my ass onto the edge of the hot tub above the deck. My skin prickles with goosebumps as my hot skin melts the bit of freezing snow that lingered there.

But I wouldn't care if I was catching hypothermia because he's already pushing my legs apart, steam lifting off our skin as he angles his cock, his eyes fixed on my pussy.

I gasp, anticipating the fullness just before he presses the bulging head inside. The guttural sound that leaves my lips is almost uncouth.

"Fuck," he exhales harshly. "Watching your pussy stretch open and take my cock will forever be burned into my memory."

He thrusts inside quickly, making my body buck as his hands grip my lower back, holding me in place.

My eyes connect with Cole's over Alec's shoulder. Those brown eyes burn into me because they're filled with all manner of filthy promises.

I can't wait.

Cole smirks like he heard my thought as he watches us from the other side of the hot tub, stroking himself.

I almost call him over, but Alec grips my chin, forcing my eyes to his.

"Keep your eyes on me, or I might get jealous."

God, I love when they do that—fight for my attention.

Alec begins fucking me slowly but only for a few decadent strokes before he pushes deep inside me, filling my tight pussy with his rock-hard cock.

We're staring at each other, locked, brimming with need. That's when the dam breaks. He hammers inside me faster and faster, with more intensity each time, eyes locked on mine. My mouth falls open, short, heaved pants leaving my body as my legs stay wrapped around his waist. We are the only two people that exist until Reed's voice breaks the bubble.

"Alec's being stingy. But I bet you want us to have a taste."

Jace's palm connects with my chest, pushing the top of my body away from Alec just as Reed grips the back of my neck.

"Yes," I rush out, seeing Alec smirk.

I'm held in place as Alec ruts into me, groaning with each motion. Reed and Jace descend upon my breasts, coming up to either side of me, wrapping their mouths around my nipples. They're teasing and licking the sensitive buds.

My eyes shift between them as I lick my lips.

Jesus Christ. I'm already there. I'm ready to come.

The tightness in my stomach grips me, making my body heat as I rock my hips to meet Alec's thrusts.

"Ah, yes. Fuck me, Alec."

He's pounding into me, over and over without mercy, and I love every minute. His cock is huge, filling me, touching every responsive spot within me, sending electric shocks through my body.

My fingers dig into the ledge as I ball my hands crushing tiny bits of snow inside my palms.

"Take me, baby. Strangle my cock," Alec grinds out between his teeth.

"You're so beautiful with your tits out. Body begging to be worshipped and used," Jace whispers in my ear.

My whimpers grow until the mewling turns into a long reverberating chant that builds from deep inside of me.

"Yes, yes, yes. Fuck me hard. Don't stop. I swear to god, don't stop, Alec."

"That's it, sunshine. Come for us. Come all over Alec's cock like a good fucking whore," Reed growls, biting my nipple.

Oh fuck.

Jace's voice follows, coaxing me closer. "I'm gonna eat that pussy and drink your fucking cum. And then we'll make it happen all over again."

My body is vibrating, shaking as I'm fucked into euphoria, screaming out an indescribable string of curses that echo into the night sky as my vision goes just as black.

Alec follows, gripping my hips hard enough to leave marks as he empties himself inside of me.

My back is arched, putting my tits on display as I enjoy the lips devouring me. My clit pulsates before I collapse into the tenderness of three men holding me.

I let out a long whoosh of breath, my eyelids feeling inescapably heavy. But before I can even attempt to open my eyes, Alec pulls out, making me gasp.

"Wait," I whine as my eyes pop open.

But my surprise turns into a smirk because my hips are attacked with a confident grip before I'm dragged back into the warmth of the water against Cole's hard body.

He dives into the crook of my neck, kissing and nibbling as we float through the water to the other side of the hot tub.

"My turn," he whispers, spinning my body around in the water so that I'm facing the bench.

My hands are gently placed on the edge of the hot tub one at a time as my knees are coaxed to find the seat. I'm kneeling, my body half out of the water, as Jace and Reed join, kissing languidly up my arms. Cole's hands glide over my ass as he stands behind me before spreading my cheeks.

"I want this. I want to eat it, fuck it and come all over it."

"Then do it," I groan, letting out a harsh exhale, and press back against him.

His thumb drags down over the tight muscle, teasing me, massaging, before pressing inside.

Jesus Christ. The underside of my breasts hit the water as my stomach contracts, and I groan unintelligible words.

"Stay still," he growls, sliding a finger inside my pussy as well.

"Oh my god," I gasp as he leans over me predatorily, biting my back before the tip of his cock replaces his thumb.

His breath hits my skin, leaving goosebumps over my wet flesh. I part my lips to moan just as Reed's lips meet mine. His tongue pushes inside my mouth, swirling, owning me before he pulls away to sit on the edge of the hot tub.

"Open wide, sunshine. Then suck."

I do as I'm told just as Cole pushes inside me, but all my moans are silenced because Reed's filling my mouth with his cock.

Reed grips the hair at the nape of my neck as he fucks my mouth.

There's something so fucking sexy about the way Reed's ass indents on the sides each time he pushes his cock into my mouth. If I could play it on a loop, I'd set it as my phone background.

I can hear him groaning above me as he picks up speed, moving in rhythm with my gagging, wiping a stray tear from my eye with his thumb.

"You like sucking my dick. Don't you? Yeah. That's so good. Hollow those fucking cheeks."

I'm humming around his dick, so turned on that I can't take anymore. Oh god. My body is begging to come again. I feel a palm skate over my breast, and I know it's Jace.

My hips are swirling, wanting more. Wanting Cole's cock inside me. But I keep my head bobbing, trying to match Reed's rhythm, even though I can barely concentrate because Cole grips my hips, moving faster.

"Fuck. I'm coming," Reed groans, mercilessly taking over fucking my swollen pout thundering, "Yes," as my mouth fills with his cum.

The moment his hand releases my head, I break away, gasping for air, and licking my lips. Cole's arm wraps around my frame, stealing me from Jace as his palm covers my breast.

Our bodies are flush as he fucks my ass, and I'm suddenly rocked by the sensation of being fucked by him.

We're so connected.

He's so fully seated inside of me that I can feel his lower stomach flex from the pleasure he feels. I lay my head back against his strong shoulders as his hands roam my body.

"Princess. I'm not going to last long inside this ass. So you're coming with me again. Now."

I'm panting, breathless, "I can't. Cole. I—"

"Shh," Jace whispers, cutting me off as he reaches under the water, adjusting the jet. I suck in a harsh breath as the powerful stream hits my clit.

"Oh my god. What the f—"

Tiny explosions begin to rumble inside of me, over and over, like the end of a fireworks show. I can't even catch my breath, let alone finish my sentence. It feels so good that I want more immediately. I'm already building, tension coiling everywhere, pressing my hips forward as Cole fucks me from behind. My lips part with harsh exhaled breaths.

"Cole. Oh. My. God—"

My words are cut off as Cole's hard cock hammers into me, chasing his release.

We're animals. Hedonists. Reduced to grunting and clawing.

Cole shoves me forward, bending me over the ledge of the hot tub so my tits are pressed against the cold surface. He's hunched over me, his arm wrapped around my stomach.

"That's it. Let me have it all, baby. Come on. Be my good girl."

The water is beating so hard against my clit that it almost stings, but the need to come overrides everything. Every muscle in my body is clenched as a silent scream possesses my body until it's thundering from my chest.

"COLE!"

I scream so loud that I can hear it inside my own head as my body convulses and doesn't stop. Even though I'm almost immediately begging for it to. Because this feeling is so overwhelming. So powerful.

"I can't," I cry. "I can't take it—"

Cole's voice is commanding and powerful as he pumps into me without any tenderness.

"More. Goddammit. You fucking taking it."

Another deep guttural bellow rips from my lips, but this time he joins me, coming inside my ass, his cock pulsating against the pressure I'm tensing with.

The jet moves away, untethering me from the elegant pain as my head bows and my body goes limp.

"Oh my god," I breathe out, blinking slowly, but Cole runs his tongue up my spine, vibrating his words against my skin as he holds me up.

"We're not done with you yet, princess. Now be a good fucking girl and open your mouth."

My heavy head lifts, vision still blurry, just as Jace's cock parts my lips. He cradles my face as he stares down at me.

"I like you used."

But I don't answer. I just hollow out my cheeks and start to suck him off.

Because the truth is, I like me used too.

twenty-two

. . .

"Hedonism is my new life aesthetic."

"We couldn't do this shit in the living room?" Reed grumbles, scowling at the space behind me on the bed taken by Cole, who's spooning me.

"You can," I snark, holding my hands out for the bowl of popcorn he's holding, adding, "No one's stopping you. I wanted to watch a movie. That didn't mean everyone had to come."

Reed rolls his eyes, tossing a piece of popcorn into his mouth before he hands me the bowl. He sits on the bed, reaching out and tugging me from Cole's hold. I plop onto my back before he lays his head down on my stomach.

I laugh, hearing Cole's huff, but I make it go away, wrapping my hand around his thigh, lifting my head, saying, "Arm, please," before feeling him slide it underneath.

"What's the name of this trash again?" Reed interjects, so I flick his ear, making him laugh.

"It's not trash. It's a cute Christmas movie about an innkeeper who's down on his luck until he meets a woman staying there, and then they fall in love."

"Sunshine, you're telling me I'm supposed to believe he's some small-town guy when that inn would value for well over two million dollars in this market. Dumb," he answers, grabbing my hand before I can injure him again, and brings it to his chest.

I counter as he nibbles the side of my palm, "Oh my god. It's romantic, Grinch. And that doesn't always mean realism. Because, see, it's fiction."

"Clearly," Cole teases. "It says the heroine is a high-powered lawyer...trying to make partner...but takes an impromptu vacation to reassess her life. Unlikely. More like she's there for a hostile takeover."

"You're a hostile takeover of my joy." I laugh. "Just shut up immediately. Because we're watching it. So zip it."

Jace chuckles, sitting at my feet, pulling them onto his lap as he extends a glass of wine my way, making my eyes light up.

"Oooo, yes, wine please. I love you."

What the fuck did I say?

I blink, stunned by my own words. I didn't mean that I loved him. Obviously, but it's awkward now that his dick's been in my ass.

"Ummm," I say, cutting the silence. "I didn't mean...I mean..." I take a breath, feeling my cheeks heat. "That's not what it sounded like...come on, that would be grounds for a restraining order. I meant it as much as when I say it to the guy at the deli because he saves me one of those extra-large pickles. You know what I mean."

I don't know why I even tried to explain because I can already tell what's about to happen.

Jace crosses his arms, his brows pulling together as he pretends to be mad.

"So, you're saying you tell every guy who feeds you an extra-large pickle that you love him?"

Oh my god. I squeeze my eyes closed for a second before I stare up at the ceiling, knowing they'll never let me live this down.

Cole dips his head toward me. "I'm hurt and frankly disappointed. You don't think my pickle is extra-large? You're a cruel woman."

Reed rolls his head toward me, a combination of mischief and bullshit written all over his stupidly gorgeous face. "And to think I thought you liked choking on my pickle."

I shake my head, kicking at Jace as I laugh. "I hate you guys. But you know what? You deserve to know that Francis owns my heart because his pickle puts all of you to shame. And it's the only one I've *never* faked choking on."

I start laughing because they all make a move like they're gearing up to pounce, but before they can, Alec walks in on his cell, grabbing our collective attention as he speaks.

"We're stocked here, so I'm not too worried. But I appreciate the call, Chief."

He hangs up, looking at the four of us cozy on the bed, and holds up the phone as if to relay who he was speaking to.

"Fire chief letting us know they won't be clearing the roads tomorrow as expected."

Wow. Tomorrow's already Monday. A tiny frown forms on my mouth. *Weekend's over.*

Alec sits in the chair next to the bed, propping his feet on the mattress.

"What the hell are we watching?"

I'm staring into space, hearing one of the guys answering him before my head turns, my eyes lagging as I face him—another thought brewing.

"When do they expect to clear the roads?"

He takes a swig of his drink before he answers me.

"They're aiming for Wednesday, gorgeous. Because more snow is expected tomorrow and Tuesday."

Oh no. I don't say that aloud. At least, I thought I didn't until four voices sound off at the same time saying the same thing.

"What's wrong?"

I shrug, feeling silly, but I answer anyway, "Tuesday's the eve of Christmas Eve."

"Or the 23rd, as the rest of the world knows it," Reed offers with a chuckle, but I click my tongue against my front teeth.

"Shut up. I mean that's the day my sister and I have this tradition where we arrive at my parents' somewhere around the crack of dawn. And we stay in our pajamas day-drinking while watching every conceivable Christmas movie. We've never missed a year together."

The look on their faces makes me want to brush away the worry because that's what they have behind their eyes. Worry. It's so sweet that I don't even know what to do with it.

"It's fine. I'm being dramatic. It's not that big of a deal."

Nobody speaks as I press play on the television, hoping to erase what I just said from everyone's memory. But I know that won't happen because I only glance at my phone before Reed sits up to nab it for me. Before treating me like a pillow again.

> **Me:** I might not be home until sometime on Tuesday night.

> **Elle:** Well, well, well. You're alive. I know you haven't even scrolled up to look at the two thousand messages I left you. Give a girl a little dick, and she forgets where she came from. Way to let the hooker fame go to your head.

I'm grinning because, in my sex fog, I forgot to message her back after the deed was done. Maybe forgot is a strong word, more like decided I wasn't telling her another word because I knew she'd want all the damn details. And I'm keeping those all to myself for just a little bit longer.

> **Me:** Omg. Quit. I told you last night I'd fill you in when I see you.

> **Elle:** I wish I had a brother. If there's anything you can count on, it's dudes sharing...PUN INTENDED.

Before I can type back, Cole steals the phone in my hands.

"No, no, no, no, no. Hold on. What are you doing?"

He has me in a loose headlock as he takes a photo of us.

"Introducing myself to your sister," he offers with no apology for reading my texts.

"Cole," I shriek, reaching for my phone, but he keeps it away from me as he types before tossing it to Reed.

"Reed," I bark. "Do not text my sister."

But he isn't listening. Reed holds the phone out, puckering his lips as he takes a selfie. Good god. Eleanor is probably in heaven.

"Hello," I yell, trying to make my smile go away, "I'm very serious. I'm going to get mad."

No acknowledgment is given other than their chuckles.

Before Reed can take another shirtless photo of himself, Jace steals my phone, briefly typing something before taking *his* selfie.

Et tu brute? That's it. I hate them.

The problem is that I don't. And the smile on my face is the dead giveaway.

Cole nuzzles my hair, pressing a kiss to my temple. I bite my lip as he says, "Think of it as proof of life since we've spent two days murdering your pussy."

"Proof of life would be photos of me, not you."

Alec hands my phone to Cole, who puts it back in my hand with a smirk. I scroll up to where Cole started the thread and almost scream-laugh. Because along with one photo after another of these idiots are bookended messages by Cole first, then Jace.

> Me: Hello, Eleanor. We apologize for stealing your sister. But I have a favor to ask. Please take these photos to Francis, the guy at her deli, and tell him his pickles are no longer needed.

> Me: Yeah and let him know if she chokes on his pickles again, I'm gonna shove all the cold cuts down his throat.

The bubbles show before Eleanor's text comes through.

> Elle: Honestly, forget Tuesday—Ask if they have brothers or friends. Maybe we should start a new tradition. One where ten lords are a leapin' into this pus—

Before I can finish reading, I drop the screen to my chest and look over at Cole, hoping he didn't see the last part. He pulls me close, kissing my forehead.

"See. Proof of life."

Wait, what? I lift my phone, quickly scrolling back up through all the pictures. But instead of noticing *them,* I see me. All the tiny pieces of me that are woven around them in every photo.

"What time is it?" I mumble, feeling someone running their knuckles up and down my jaw from behind. "Or maybe I should say, what day is it?"

"Monday."

I turn around with my coffee cup in hand to see Alec's smiling face.

"Hi," I whisper.

"The sun's almost up, gorgeous. Follow me. I have something I've been meaning to show you."

I take a sip of my coffee, sliding my hand into his without question. I knew it was early, but I hadn't bothered to check the time before crawling out between the guys and making myself a coffee.

It's part of my new go-with-the-flow attitude. I figure hedonism is my new life aesthetic.

I follow behind him as my eyes shift past the floor-to-ceiling windows in the living room. With all the lights off, you can see the snow falling outside. It's slower than I expected since the roads couldn't be cleared but still beautiful and quiet in that magical Christmas movie way.

I shiver. Alec looks over his shoulder.

"Cold," I whisper.

"Blankets," he whispers back, swiping two off the couch.

Alec wraps the crimson cashmere around me, snuggling it up under my chin before smiling at me. We stand there in silence, only our collective breathing, the only thing giving away our presence.

Alec's lips part as if he's about to speak, but the moment is interrupted by my stomach growling.

Alec's eyebrows raise as my shoulders shake with laughter.

"Do we need to feed you again, gorgeous? You weren't lying when you said you had a healthy appetite."

I shake my head, lifting to my tiptoes.

"I'm not hungry for food, Alec."

He smiles against my lips, kissing me gently.

"Maybe we should do that thing you seemed to like the other night."

I nod, biting my lip as I drop back to my heels. Knowing exactly what he's talking about.

We'd only made it halfway through the movie before someone made a move. I'm not even sure who touched who first—me or Reed. But I do know that I found myself straddling him, reverse cowgirl, as Alec became very well acquainted with the back of my throat before he came down it.

The best part was when Alec did, he looked me directly in the eyes, saying nothing. And I swear I could see reverence in them. After he finished, he gently swiped his thumb over my used lips, ensuring I was left as clean as I began before whispering, "You're perfect."

It was so sexy and adoring that the moment burned itself into my mind.

I blink, staring up into his bright eyes, into all the little specks of blues that mix with a streak of green. Just like that, the quietest thought in the recesses of my brain begins to yell at me.

You like him. You like them.

Oh fuck.

Oh fuck.

There would be no mixing business with pleasure, Samantha. You're here for the weekend. That's it. That's what we all agreed to. It's not like I could date them. I mean...I can't...right?

Oh my god. Why did I even pause on that thought?

Dating four guys at the same time is only for reality television shows that hand out roses, and romance novels. Not real life. A few days ago I was having a small panic attack over the idea of sleeping with them but now I'm going to date them? Yeah, right.

But therein lies the problem. It's only been three days, and the bar for men has already been moved to an Olympics kind of high. Like the kind of high you see and think, "Yeah, someone might die making it over that bar."

God, I can't like them this way. Because what the hell am I going to do after I leave? Redo my Tinder profile to say: *Must-have—friends I can fuck and who like to cook for me. Will also let me talk endlessly about how I'd redo their kitchen layout. Bonus if you have shitty taste in movies but are willing to sit through cheesy romantic comedies debating the reality of character career choices. And please have excellently timed water jet skills in the Jacuzzi.*

And make me laugh, feel worshipped and play with locks of my hair like Alec is doing right now as he stares down at me.

Shit. No. Once the roads are clear, we will go our separate ways, sexually speaking. Oh Jesus, how am I going to work with them again?

I'm so fucked. Or maybe it's fine...yeah, it'll be fine. Sucking off all a guy's friends automatically excludes you from being his plus-one...two, three, *and* four. But choosing paint colors is fine. Until it's not.

This is the worst. I mean, what did I even think could happen? That I'd put the guys in my calendar like the moon cycles? Reed's dick is waning while Jace's is waxing? Whatever the fuck that means.

But then again, I guess I could take a dick break for my period during the blood moon. Eww, Jesus, why am I like this? This is no time for humor. I'm literally trying to figure out how to polyamory with four dudes who just wanted to fuck me for a weekend.

How fucking starved was my pussy? One dirty dip, and she's a crack whore.

Crack is wack. Whitney said so. I've got to get my shit together. Maybe first I should stop pretending that this is all about sex. It may have started that way, but I fear I've caught an STD of the heart, and no amount of penicillin will cure it.

My eyes search Alec's, my mouth tipping up into a grin entertained by my rambling thoughts as he sweeps my hair behind my ear before pressing a kiss to my forehead.

"I don't even want to ask what you're thinking, do I?" I bite my lip. Shaking my head as he adds, "Come on."

I tug his hand, still following. "Are you going to tell me what we're doing, or am I supposed to guess?"

He just grins, walking toward Jace's room. So I tug his hand again.

"I thought we were recreating last night. Doesn't that mean we should wake everyone up?"

"This is just for us." He smiles back over his shoulder before leading me straight into the bedroom.

My brows furrow, clumsy words tumbling out.

"Wait, why are we in Jace's room? And more importantly, are we allowed to do this?"

Alec shuts the door behind us, pausing for a moment, tilting his head.

"He has the best view…and do what, exactly?"

My eyes widen, trying to make him catch on. But he just raises his brows.

"You know…" I lower my voice for whatever reason. "Have sex without the others. Is that, like, breaching our contract?"

"I don't remember signing anything."

Jerk. He's teasing, but my question is valid. My hand darts out, wrapped in a handful of the blanket as I playfully push his chest.

"Come on. You know what I mean."

He takes my hands, leaning down and kissing me before speaking.

"We've never done this, sweetheart…spent more than one night with a woman. We barely know the women we —" I feel the frown, so I know he sees it. But he smirks. "Let's just say that *this*—our time here with you—is unexplored territory."

Why is my heart beating so fast? And why am I about to say the thing I know better than to say? Still, I don't even try to stop the words from tumbling out.

"Do you wish we could explore it, though?"

That question reeks of complication and a foregone conclusion of a no, but I don't take it back.

I think it's because the way he's looking at me makes me want to know if he likes me the way I like him. Kind of like when you're in middle school, and you let your friend concoct a note to pass with boxes to check for yes and no.

Check yes, Alec.

Alec looks back over his shoulder, and my eyes drop to his cheek, noticing the streak of light spreading across it.

"Yeah," he whispers, pulling me against him, turning us toward the window as the room illuminates with the most vibrant pinks and oranges as the sunrise makes its grand entrance. "I do, Samantha."

twenty-three

· · ·

"Merry eve of Christmas Eve, baby."

"**W**hy are you up…blocking the door, Reed?" I say with a grin walking out of the bathroom.

I'd taken a shower after my much-needed and very long nap this afternoon—which he is partially at fault for, seeing as how they revel in exhausting me. But last I left him, he was still lying on the bed. Asleep next to me.

He smirks, crossing his arms and leaning back against the heavy oak door.

"Because there's something we don't want you to see yet. And now that you're finally awake, we can do the loud parts." He rolls his eyes for added humor, saying, "Obviously. Now be good and cooperate, sunshine."

I scowl, but he motions toward the bed. "Let's put on one of those dumpster-fire movies you like so much."

"That *you* like too," I shoot back, dropping my towel and watching him bite his lip. But I pretend to be unaffected as I throw on yet another T-shirt as I add, "I saw you browsing when I got out of the shower."

Reed smirks. "I was looking for porn. I figured we could find more kinky revelry you might like."

I squint my eyes just as the sounds of banging echo from the living room. He just shrugs and winks. So I pad across the carpet quickly toward him. Completely unable to hide my smile.

"Reed," I whine in only the cutest way. "Tell me what's going on, and I'll be your best friend."

He chuckles. "I already have three." I scowl, but he taps my nose. "Look at you, a fiend for ruining surprises." His head tilts to the side. "You could always try to beat it out of me."

I laugh because he adjusts himself as he says it. His eyes drop down my body as he goes to grab for me, but I take a step back, staying just out of reach.

"Naughty girl," he croons. "If you want out, you'll have to barter for your freedom."

Our eyes are connected as I swallow hard because Reed is just so fucking Reed.

"Oh, cut to the chase. What do you want?" I whisper, body almost vibrating with anticipation.

"There's not much I don't want."

He pushes off the door, grabbing a handful of my shirt before tugging me flush to him as he reaches back and locks the door. My chest rises and falls, eyes closed as he dips his lips to my neck.

Wait, what was I asking for? Or was he asking for something? Oh, who cares.

Two knocks bang against the door just as he forces my

head to the side, giving himself more room to devour my neck. My shoulders jump before I shove my palms against his chest, pushing him back. But Reed only lifts his mouth to yell, "Fuck off. We'll be out in a minute," as he tugs me back against him.

I smile as my arms wrap around his neck, laughter filling the air. His lips descend back on mine as his hands drag up the sides of my face into my hair. Reed kisses the hell out of me. Stealing all my breath and cutting off any humor left in me.

"Mmmm," I moan into his mouth, my body feeling pliable, molding itself to him. But I'm jerked from the decadence hearing Jace's voice bellow through the locked door.

"Reed. If you don't get the fuck off my girl..."

"My girl," Reed growls into my mouth.

I love when they fight over me.

I'm laughing into the kiss, but Reed's already walking us backward toward the bed. He's either going to fuck me while they listen or that door is getting knocked down. I'm betting the latter.

There's more banging mixed with Cole saying something about finding a key or a chainsaw before I'm hauled directly onto the bed.

"Reed," I squeal, laughing harder as cursing comes from outside.

He reaches over his shoulder and drags his shirt over his head, looking down at me with a smirk.

"It's gonna take them a few minutes to find the key that opens your door. I say we get started without them."

I don't say a word. But my legs spread. Pussy already

glistening, inviting everything he wants to give, as I bite my lip and look up innocently.

"Damn, that's pretty," he exhales all gravelly.

Goosebumps erupt all over me as his palms hit the mattress, and he crawls toward me. But just as my mouth opens for me to speak, Reed dives between my legs, holding them open. He swipes his tongue flat over my clit, making me tremble before he sucks on it gently.

"Oh my god," I gasp, falling back onto the bed, my fingers weaving through his sexy tousled hair. "You're so good at that."

He lifts his face, mouth glistening, biting at my wrist playfully. "Come on, sunshine. You can do better than that. How about *Reed, you're the god of pussy. Or Reed, make me—*"

"Shut up," I snark, cutting him off, pushing his face back to where it belongs.

He growls, hooking his arms around my legs, but I'm smiling because Alec is laughing from the other side of the door as Cole tosses out threats.

"I knew we shouldn't have agreed to let you keep her busy. I'm going to leave you outside to fucking freeze to death if that girl comes without my cock inside her."

Reed grins. "Looks like Daddy's mad. Sunshine, would you like to see how he'll punish you for being bad?" He bites the inside of my thigh. "Because I would."

I laugh, totally owned by this sexual mischief.

My chin lifts as I run my hands up my body, bringing my shirt with it, exposing my breasts as I yell, "You better hurry, Cole. Reed is very good at being bad."

That's all it takes. I'm attacked. Reed's tongue moves in

figure-eights around my clit, switching between long strokes up my folds. Jesus, I'm a five-star meal. My hips circle as I squeeze my ass, pressing myself closer to his face, the sound of begging mewls tumbling from between my lips.

"Fuck me. I'm going to kill him," someone outside the room groans, then Jace's voice makes me shiver.

"Cutie, don't listen to Cole. I might come just hearing you. Don't hold back...I wanna hear every fucking lick and moan."

Jesus, that's sexy.

Reed's fingers dig into my thighs as he begins rhythmically sucking on my clit, before alternating between flicking his tongue over and over, relentlessly owning my pussy.

I'm breathless, climbing higher, wanting more and more.

I grip the sheets, grinding into his face, feeling my stomach tighten.

"Yes. Reed, don't stop."

"Reed," Alec bellows.

Reed's tongue thrusts inside me before slowly gliding up over every ridge and crease of my wet pussy.

"Oh god," I groan, then laugh as more banging echoes.

Reed holds me tighter, coaxing me closer to bliss as he growls his words against my center.

"Don't come yet, sunshine. I want to feel it happen."

"Reed," I breathe out. "I'm too close—" But I don't finish what I'm saying because his lips are already moving up my stomach.

Reed crawls on top of me, engulfing me with his lean

muscular body. He's staring down at me with those deep green eyes as he slides a hand down between us. I gasp, my eyes closed as he slides two fingers inside my cunt and whispers, "Gimme. I want that pussy to cry for me."

We're sealed against each other as he starts to finger me slowly. All the sound from outside the room goes still, and suddenly, Reed and I are in our own bubble.

"Look at me," he says quietly.

My eyes flicker open to his again as my lips part. Our breath is matched, ragged and raw as he begins gliding in and out of my slick center. His eyes never leaving mine.

Something shifts between us.

Because he's looking back at me with the same look I'm sure I have on my face. It's the one where we wish this was real. That he was mine and I was his.

Problem is, I want all of them. And that's precisely why I will love and hate this weekend until the end of time.

The palm of his hand is creating friction with my clit as he gently brushes his lips over my cheeks.

We're quiet. Lost in each other as my body rocks with the motion of his fingers curled inside me. His voice drifts over me, leaving goosebumps up my neck.

"You feel so good." He swallows. "Sunshine... you...this..."

He doesn't finish, looking the most lost I've ever seen him. All his regular confidence is stripped bare as he stares down at me. My breath becomes ragged, and my hands grip his biceps as we stay so connected that it makes me almost say something foolish.

"I wish—" *I could keep all of you.*

Our lips meet because I'm a coward. But he pulls away,

dipping in to kiss me once more as we rock faster, my body chasing what it craves. His hand moving faster, fingers fucking me as my swollen clit begins to throb with need.

"You wish?" he presses. "Say it, sunshine. Tell me what you wish."

Don't. You'll ruin this.

"I wish for another day. Just one more," I say in a whoosh as I come, quietly shaking, holding on to him as he kisses me violently.

I'm panting as he snuggles his head into the crook of my neck but all too soon, and well before I'm ready, I'm left cold.

Reed's off the bed before I can stop him, retreating toward the door, running his hand through his hair as he keeps his back to me.

"Reed?" I say quietly, but he looks back over his shoulder with that perfectly patented smirk just as the sound of the door unlocking fills the room.

Smirking faces become Reed's backdrop as he winks at me.

"Come on, sunshine. Fun's over. We've got a surprise for you...it is the eve of Christmas Eve, after all."

I CAN'T SPEAK. OR MOVE. OR ANYTHING. I JUST KEEP LOOKING around the living room as I squeeze Reed's hand. The one that hasn't stopped holding mine ever since we walked out of the bedroom.

"You guys," I breathe out, smiling.

Mismatched sheets are strung up like sails around the living room, making a cozy tent just big enough for the five of us. It's adorned with twinkle lights stolen from the tree, and inside the tent is quite possibly every fluffy pillow and cashmere blanket in this house.

Oh my god, they even have popcorn and wine in there. It's the most magical thing I've ever seen.

I let go of Reed's hand, bringing mine to my neck, feeling the flush growing. I'm so overwhelmed that I'm almost speechless. My face shifts to Reed's.

"You built me a grown-up-sized fort."

He grins. "Technically, *they* built it while *I* made you come."

My palms land on his chest, steadying me as I lift to my tiptoes and kiss his chin.

"Thank you for doing your part."

He grins as Jace takes my hand, leading me closer to the sheet-swept entrance.

"Cutie, you were so disappointed about the possibility of missing out on your tradition, we thought we'd bring it to you."

Alec tucks my hair behind my ear, kissing my forehead and adding, "There's a television inside. For all your Christmas movie needs. And your sister is waiting for you to FaceTime her. She's been waiting most of the day, but we didn't want to wake you."

"What?" I exhale.

I blink, lowering my head to see the soft glow of a movie already playing before shifting between them. My mouth opens then closes, not knowing what to say.

"This is... I don't know what to say... You are the sweetest men. Thank you."

I'm smiling so bright I bet it could be seen through the window. Cole steps closer, taking my hand and kissing the top.

"Merry Christmas, baby."

twenty-four

• • •

"Do they even have missing kid pictures on the
side of milk anymore?"

I t's almost pitch-black sans the glow from the one
strand of Christmas lights we left on, coupled with
the wink from the sun as it starts to rise. The fire
went out ages ago, but our den of sin has kept me warm. I
take a quiet deep breath, feeling too much.

It's officially Christmas Eve.

I anticipated feeling down after missing the kickoff of
my family festivities. But that's not what I feel because last
night left its mark.

After Eleanor and I watched one of our favorites, she
made Jace show her his tattoos. She's such a whore. But
the guys indulged her, making both of us laugh. They even
sat and listened as we speculated about who'd get the
sloppiest at Christmas dinner this year—our train wreck of
an uncle or our grandmother who still wears six-inch heels
at the age of eighty-five. The more she drinks, the more she
leans until she's the living embodiment of the Leaning
Tower of Pisa. Nobody knows how she doesn't topple.

Even with all the embarrassing stories, the night was perfect, actually better, because the moment I ended the call, I was fucked, twice.

I smile thinking about it. And thinking about how much we laughed. It was a ridiculous amount. If this were a movie, this would be when they cut to the flashback showing us throwing popcorn as Alec hauled me into his lap to use me as a shield.

We'd be a replica of happiness. The kind of couple goals everyone hides on their secret Pinterest boards. The only difference is that my photo has four guys.

Another long breath breezes past my lips.

"Fuck," I whisper, staring at the tiny bulb of blurred-out light, adjusting my head closer to Cole's arm.

Jace's arm slips around my waist, his naked body flush with my back. His deep voice whispers from behind, pulling me from my thoughts.

"Why are you up?"

I roll over. Our faces are so close that it's almost hard to focus on his.

"Hi," I whisper dreamily.

He smiles, rubbing his nose against mine before pulling back.

"So, are you going to tell me what's on your mind?"

"Nothing." I grin.

"Oh, come on, I may not have history with you, but here's what I know from this weekend. When you're nervous, you ramble." I chuckle, snuggling closer as he speaks, even though my arms are folded against my chest. "And when you're thinking, you're quiet, you lock your-self away with your thoughts. But wild thoughts are always going on inside that mind of yours—they're practically written all over your face."

"No, they aren't."

He smirks. "You, cutie, are an open book."

A small frown grows on my face. "That's funny. My whole life, I've been told the opposite. My sister always says I'm unreadable."

Jace kisses me sweetly. "Then I'm happy you let your guard down. Because you're pretty fucking amazing."

One kiss turns into another, then another, until he pulls away just as breathless as I am. His eyes are shining back to mine. He's looking at me like I'm Christmas morning as he exhales my name.

"Sammy." His hand sweeps over my cheek, cradling my face. "What are you doing to me? My head is fucked-up over you."

I blink. Trying to swallow all the words I haven't said. The feeling that's been growing inside me to tell them what I wish could happen between us. Even in my best efforts, those words stay settled on the tip of my tongue, brimming.

"Mine too," I answer honestly, still managing to deceive him.

Jace's fingers weave through my hair as he runs his other hand down my body, hitching my leg over his hip. I can feel every inch of him pressed against me, wanting me as I want him. But we lay there silently looking at each other until his perfect lips part.

"I want you...I—" He exhales, then pauses, closing his eyes.

I finally understand what "waiting with bated breath"

means because there's more to that sentence. And it's making everything feel like the edge of a cliff. *Just say it, Jace.* But instead of finishing that sentence, he kisses me.

He presses his lips to mine, and I take it. Because we both know that we aren't something that can happen in the real world. *We* are only for sexy magical weekends packed with long snow days. And that's that.

So when Jace opens his mouth again, I seal it to mine. Saving us the regret as I grind into him, moaning as his hand covers my breast.

"Fuck me," I rasp. "I want you inside of me, Jace."

"Samantha," he growls, moving his mouth along my jaw.

We're writhing against each other as another hand squeezes my ass, and I feel a hard cock grind against it.

"Cole," I say in a whoosh of breath, feeling Jace push his dick inside me.

Cole growls in my ear, "Looks like I woke up just in time to fuck this sweet little ass again."

"Yes, please," I rasp.

Jace's hips thrust forward slowly, savoring every second of our connection as I wrap my arms around his neck, not wanting to let go. Because I'm going to have to. Whether it's today or tomorrow, I will have to let go of this tiny slice of heaven and go back to the real world.

My eyes are closed, and my body is already damp with sweat because I'm sandwiched between Cole and Jace. They take turns kissing my neck and shoulders, their hands running all over my body. I feel Cole's cock begin to rim my ass, and desire takes over. My back arches, jutting my ass toward him as Jace slides his cock in and out in a torturous tempo.

"Pull out," Cole grunts.

I gasp at the loss of Jace's cock as Cole reaches between my legs and gathers the wetness, pushing his fingers inside of me before spreading it back over my ass.

"Relax for him, baby," Jace whispers into my lips, kissing me deeply as the head of his cock pushes back inside my pussy.

I gasp, feeling like my body is on fire.

Cole's hand grips my hip, positioning himself behind me, but my eyes spring open. My mouth tearing away from Jace's as my head shifts toward the opening of our sheet fort.

"Did you hear that? Was that the—"

My eyes grow wide. And all the hands drop from my body.

Jace gently removes my leg as he sits up, mirroring Cole. They're pulling on their pants as the sound rings again.

Holy hell.

"It's the doorbell," I say, almost angry.

Cole hands me his shirt. "Cover up, baby."

It rings again. And this time, Reed and Alec wake up, hurrying their clothes on and kissing me before they join Cole and Jace at the door. But I'm still sitting in the tent, brows drawn together as I listen to Alec greet the Fire Chief.

I slide the shirt I'm holding over my head, inhaling the scent of Cole as I adjust it over my shoulders.

What the hell is wrong with me? It's freaking

Christmas Eve. And we've finally been saved. I can go home and be with my family. Sleep in my own bed. Shave my legs...and my...

I'll be honest. I've been on borrowed time. My well-shorn lady bits were about to turn into a 1970s bush.

Still. I don't move.

The sheets swish open, Alec's face coming into view.

"You're clear. Come on."

He holds out his hand for me to take, and I do, letting him help me out. But as soon as I'm exposed, four sets of eyes stare down at me, unspeaking.

I swallow, already knowing the answer to my question.

"I take it we've been sprung from snow jail?"

Alec clears his throat. "It would seem so. The chief said they've finished most of the mountain."

I'm nodding. But there's more silence. My fingers find the hem of my shirt...I mean, Cole's shirt that I'm borrowing because the weekend is officially over. I bite the inside of my cheek before I speak, hoping for a Hail Mary.

"But are the roads still icy?"

Cole shakes his head, cutting me off quickly. "No. It's all good, Samantha. We can leave whenever we'd like. It's our choice, now."

"Oh."

Right. Our choice...the one we agreed to for the time we were snowed in. God. This is so embarrassing. I must look like an idiot to them, like a lovesick puppy. This was for the weekend. And that's officially over.

"Cool," I breathe out, shooting off finger guns. *Jesus, not this again.* How could I regress this quickly back to the pre-fivesome me? Maybe because I just had Jace inside me and

Cole on deck. And now I'm being ejected, tossed back into reality.

I'm walking backward away from them and the tent, unable to shut my horrendous diarrhea mouth.

"The timing is perfect, actually. Because you guys probably have stuff to do. And people to get back to—"

They're not speaking, just watching me fumble my words. And I don't stop.

"—I mean, let's be real. One more day and my parents would've probably sent out an Amber Alert. Wanted proof of life. Next thing I know, I'd be on the side of milk cartons. Amiright?"

My legs hit the coffee table, causing me to squeal as my ass hits the top of it before I rebound back to standing.

"Sorry. I mean...the table doesn't care. You probably don't either. Jesus," I breathe out, cheeks red as I smooth my hands over my errant hair.

Reed steps forward, followed by Jace, but I shake my head. "I'm fine. Totally good in the hood. Oh my god, I don't know why I said that."

I turn around, mouth dry, cheeks red, hearing Cole say my name. But all that comes out of my mouth is, "Do they even have missing kid pictures on the side of milk anymore? I'm kind of lactose intolerant, so I wouldn't really know anyway."

"Samantha," he presses, forcing me to turn around.

Fuck me. They're looking at me like they don't know what to do with me. *Fair, guys. Me neither.*

"I'm gonna go...change out of this T-shirt...and then head home." *Someone stop me.* "Because the storm is over."

Say something. "So there's no real reason for me to stay." *Just say you want me to.*

The last part of what I said hangs in the middle of the room until Cole's eyes lock on mine.

"You can leave the shirt on the bed."

I don't stick around to answer. No, I power walk like a suburban fifty-something in the 1980s back to my fucking room and shut the door behind me.

I lift the phone I don't even remember grabbing, swiping it open to text my sister.

> Me: Good news. I'm free.

> Elle: Ha. Free? Put me in your jail. Should I tell Mom to expect four more?

> Me: No. The weekend's over. And so are we.

Bubbles. Then nothing. Then bubbles again.

> Elle: FaceTime?

> Me: No. I'll see you soon. Put two bottles in the chiller for me.

> Elle: For just you?

> Me: Yeah—blackout drunk seems like a real good idea.

twenty-five

. . .

"We all just turned into a bunch of jackasses."

alec

She's been gone for all of five minutes, but none of us have left the spot we stood in as she said goodbye. I never thought in a million years that not one of us would have enough fucking balls to tell the girl we liked her. But that's exactly what we did. We stood here in a fucking receiving line and let her say goodbye.

Fuck. I close my eyes, thinking about the all-too-fresh moment.

"Do you have everything?" Forget something, so you'll have to come back.

She nods. "I didn't have much to start with."

Stay, gorgeous.

She blinks up, placing her hand on my shoulder as she lifts to kiss my cheek.

"Thanks for a wonderful weekend. Since it was literally my pleasure."

252

I huff a laugh, wanting to pull her back and wrap her in a hug, then tell her she's staying whether she likes it or not.

She sidesteps to stand in front of Jace. My eyes tick to his face, recognizing that look. He doesn't want her to go either. Fuck. I'm pretty sure he hasn't even heard a word she's said to him. Because the minute she kisses his cheek, shifting her face toward Reed, I swear Jace looks more deflated than I've ever seen him.

And I was there the year he lost the Super Bowl.

But we still have Reed. If there's anyone that won't respect her wishes, it's him. It won't matter that she said there was no reason for her to stay—he'll find one.

She's smiling up at him, but his jaw is tense. What the fuck? What's wrong with him?

She calls him close, forcing him to bend, so she can whisper in his ear. His eyes close before a thin veil of bullshit closes over him. Protecting himself from her seeing what I do.

That he likes her too.

Double fuck.

Her hand lingers on his chest before she moves to Cole. But in true fashion, he takes control of the moment, taking her hand and kissing it before leading her to the door.

The cold drifts in as it opens, and she looks back at us—a bunch of fucking emotional grown-ass-man chickens. She gives a small wave accompanied by an even smaller smile. And then she's gone.

My hands run through my hair as I finally step away from where I've felt rooted, letting the moment fall from my mind. Jace's voice follows me.

"What now?"

Reed clears his throat before answering.

"Now we pack up. And get out of here."

Jace crosses his arms. "Are we really pretending we're not rocked by that shit? By that girl? We all just turned into a bunch of jackasses."

Cole's jaw tenses. "We made a deal, Jace. And the deal is done. If she wanted to amend it, we gave her plenty of room to do that. Not crossing a line *she set* doesn't make us jackasses."

"Bullshit," Jace spits. "We should've said something. Given her the option at least."

"For what?" Reed bellows, throwing his hands in the air. "To date us? Have you even thought about how that would work? Because I fucking have. Who goes first? Who does she introduce to her family? Her friends? Or do we just show out together because that won't cause a scene? The weekend is over, J. It doesn't matter how we feel. We're going home. And then you can find a little piece to bury your dick in and get over it."

Hands connect with chests, and before I know it, Reed and Jace are tussling like a bunch of assholes. Fuck-yous are hurled left and right. But Cole and I are there in an instant, pulling them off each other.

"Enough," I thunder.

My voice cuts through the bullshit as they look at me.

"We need to shut the house down and get back to the city. Because we can't do shit about the *what-ifs* since we're here and she's there."

Jace and Reed disperse, Reed chucking something in his hand out of frustration. But that's not my concern anymore. Right now, it's Cole who's looking at the door.

My hand falls heavy on his shoulder.

"She's one of a kind."

He says nothing but he doesn't have to. So I keep talking.

"The weekend was always going to be enough...or not. We knew that going in."

Cole huffs a laugh.

"We're fucked, Alec. Because if there's a possibility to keep her...I'm not so sure I'm willing to share. And I'd venture to bet we'd each say the same."

A smirk grows on my face. "Then I guess negotiations should start in the car...where we can't kill each other."

twenty-six

· · ·

"My life is not a book, Eleanor."

"We're so glad to have you home," my mom breathes.

I smile at my mom and nod as my sister pours a very generous glass of white wine for me.

We've been holed up in the kitchen pretending to help my mom cook. My dad walks past me, giving my back a gentle pat.

"Yeah, Mom was starting to think we'd never get you back off that mountain."

I take a gulp before shrugging.

"Well, I'm back in one piece..." *Kind of.*

He momentarily frowns at me, but my sister just tops off my glass, interjecting, "Did I tell you I started dating that guy—"

"Which guy?" Mom shoots back, looking up from the bowl she's mixing stuffing ingredients in.

Eleanor leans on the counter, giving me a wink. "The one from the roller derby. He's so hot."

My dad scoffs.

"The one with a purple mohawk and all the metal in his face? Jesus Christ. It must take him an hour to go through airport security."

My mother chuckles but Eleanor shrugs.

"He doesn't believe in flying...he's reducing his carbon footprint."

I almost laugh because it's like she customized the perfect story to set our retired airline pilot father off and away from my bummed-out mood.

My phone buzzes in the pocket of my cardigan before I pull it out, staring down at the texts.

"I'll be right back," I barely say audibly before slipping off the kitchen stool to go somewhere more private.

Four texts stare back at me.

They must've all sent them at the same time without telling each other they were doing it.

> Cole: Home?

> Jace: You good?

> Reed: Proof of life? Naked pics, preferably.

> Alec: Got home safe?

"Wow," my sister rushes out from behind me, resting her chin on my shoulder to look at my messages. "I call bullshit. Those guys are interested. You sooo predictably read them wrong."

I shake my head, thumbs hovering.

"I know they like me, Elle. But…I like *them*. Emphasis on *them*. And they don't do that."

She scurries in front of me, grabbing my thumbs so that I can't text.

"How is it you managed to find a pack of emotionally unavailable fuck boys?"

I roll my eyes. "I'm just lucky, I guess."

"Wait, how do you know they don't do that?"

I scowl. "Because they laid it out at the start."

She tugs my hands. "But you said Alec said it was unexplored territory. Did you ever just tell them what you wanted?"

I shake my head. And she laughs.

"Why are you so dumb? God, I hate this trope."

"My life is not a book, Eleanor. Cole walked me to the door. Reed didn't say anything. None of them did. I made a fool of myself, standing there waiting for them to say anything to stop me. If he wants to, he will—isn't that the saying? Well, they obviously didn't want to. So—"

She pulls me into a hug. "I'm sorry."

I pout. "It's fine. I'll get over it. It's not like we're in love. I just…"

Eleanor releases me, smiling as she draws back, and finishes my sentence, "Wanted your own boy band?"

"Yeah," I sigh.

She turns to rejoin my parents in the kitchen, motioning for me to come too. But my eyes drop to my phone, teeth finding my lip as I make a group message.

> Me: I'm home. Miss you guys.

No, *delete, delete, delete.*

> Me: I'm home. Let's get drinks soon.

No, we can't do that. Shit. *Delete, delete, delete, delete.*

> Me: I'm home. And, ummm, I think I quit.

twenty-seven

. . .

"Wait...she dated all of them...at the same time?"

"**A**re you having fun?" my sister snarks, knowing my answer as she raises her phone for yet another selfie of us to put on the 'Gram.

"Define fun." I chuckle, taking another sip of the cheap champagne.

I look around at all the people dressed to the nines, here in this damn ballroom ready to greet the New Year, and I'm still stuck on this year. I should've said no to this stupid party when my sister forced it on me. But I was desperate to get them off my mind.

Because that's where Alec, Reed, Jace, and Cole have been. The only place actually, because after I sent the "I quit" text, there's been nothing but radio silence.

Why did I do that? It was symbolic really. It's not like I work for them, but I also can't work with them anymore. That would be torture.

God, is it too much to expect for them to disregard what I'm saying on the surface and focus on what they should psychically know? I laugh to myself, taking another sip of my drink before placing it on the cocktail table I'm standing next to.

My sister rubs her shoulder against mine.

"Buck up. At least your date is adorable. He even bought an *Architectural Digest* to learn about all the dumb shit you're interested in."

I shrug, scrunching my nose. She shoves my shoulder playfully.

"You're such a bitch, Sam. Not every guy has three friends he'll let fuck you. And you never know, maybe he's good and hung."

Gross.

"I have zero interest in fucking him, Eleanor." I narrow my eyes on her. "You didn't tell him I would when you set us up, did you?"

Her mouth drops open. "What kind of person do you think I am?"

"The kind you are. I'm going to kill you."

She laughs. "I said you were adventurous. And you are..." She gives me a knowing look. "Plus, I peeped at his Instagram. He has some fine-ass friends. You could do a little product comparison."

She's wagging her eyebrows, but I'm shaking my head.

"Oh my god. I hate you. I am not going to fuck Cole just so I can compare him to Jace. You are truly feral."

She deadpans. Staring at me deeply, lifting her glass to her shiny red lips before she smirks.

"Your date's name is Christopher."

My eyes grow wide as my lips press together to hold

back my smile. *Shit. I totally said Cole.* But I scoff, trying to play it cool.

"What? That's what I said."

Her long fingernail jabs my bare shoulder. "No, you said Cole…as in Cole who spit on your—"

I shove her drink against her lips forcing liquid down her throat, making her choke and laugh while swatting me away.

"I'm pressing charges," she coughs out, making me laugh.

"Fuck," I breathe out roughly. "I'm so fucked. I'm literally always thinking about them. It's so embarrassing to be the girl hung up on the guy who doesn't like her back."

"Four guys."

"Okay," I bark.

Her bottom lip pops out. And I shrug before looking over my shoulder for our dates.

"Where did they go to get us drinks?"

"Who cares? Don't deflect. I say just text them. Do a group chat. Since ya did a group fuck."

"No," I say, shaking my head and staring back at her like she's lost it. "It was for the weekend. I need to get over it."

"Come on." She laughs. "You're being ridiculous. People have polyamorous relationships all the time. You're not that unique."

My brows draw together. "Yeah, on communes…where they grow corn that weird children live in."

She laughs at my movie reference, and I follow, rubbing my lips together before she takes my hand.

"I just think you should go with your heart, wherever it takes you."

I squeeze her hand and smile.

"You know, sometimes you're halfway decent, and I almost like you."

My sister's face stills, eyes growing wide.

"What?" I tease. "This is your one compliment a year."

Her smile starts to grow and something about it makes my stomach start to flip. Her eyes dart back to mine, holding me hostage as she says, "If you have ever taken any advice from me, now is the time."

My voice sounds as terrified as I am as I draw out, "Whyyy?"

"Because they're here," she whispers. "All four of them."

My face swings to look over my shoulder, but she nearly slaps it back to hers.

"This is your moment. Say what you want, bitch. You want them? Then get them. But make them work for it."

I'm nodding. But at what? Because I don't even know what she said. My head is exploding. And my mouth is so dry that I can barely swallow. I wish I could say something cute and dainty like butterflies swarmed in my stomach, but this feels more like my heart is about to drop out of my ass.

"Pay attention," she hisses.

Oh god, I can't listen to her. She's the same person that convinced me to dress as a Dalmatian to her Cruella for three years in a row when we were kids.

I'm panicking, still in my head, as I whisper, "Cruella wanted to skin the puppies."

Eleanor points her finger in my face.

"What the fuck are you talking about? Listen to me. You are dating Christopher—he's fucking delicious and does things to you that not even *they* can imagine."

"What? Wait. Why?"

But she doesn't answer as she spins me around laughing, eyes glancing, head tilting, like I should do the same. So I do, but it sounds more like I'm crying.

What the fuck is happening?

"Are you okay?" comes from my side as Christopher walks back holding two drinks.

Oh god.

I swipe a champagne from him, rushing out, "I'm so sorry for what's about to happen," before I down the glass and switch it out with the other one in his hand.

He's staring at me, probably about to ask what the hell is wrong with me, when we're suddenly surrounded. At least, that's what it feels like. Because my favorite set of eyes...all four of them...are staring directly at me.

There's a whole party happening around me. People laughing, dancing in ballgowns, and drinking champagne as they ready for the countdown. But I'm standing in the spotlight of their attention. Unable and unwilling to break away.

Christopher clears his throat, extending his hand to Reed.

"Hi, I'm Christopher, Samantha's—"

But Reed cuts him off with a singular, "Nope."

I smirk, putting my hands on my hips.

"What are you guys doing here? I'm on a date."

Christopher raises his hand as if to claim the title, but Jace lowers it for him.

Alec crosses his arms, glancing at the guys before he narrows his eyes on me.

"You left us. We want an explanation."

Heat rises through my body. Are they fucking kidding?

"Wait a minute. How did you know I was here?"

Alec grins, looking at Reed who lifts his chin toward my sister, saying, "I follow her on Instagram."

Damn you, Elle. I will kill her later.

Alec's unwavering glare calls to me, locking my gaze back on him.

"Well?" he presses.

"Well, what?" I snap back.

His giant body feels foreboding as he takes a step closer.

"We left our annual New Year's party to come here. We left a hundred or so guests, for an answer, gorgeous, and we're not leaving until we get one."

I scowl, shooting my words with impeccable aim. "You didn't ask me to stay. It's that simple."

Reed steps in closer. "What if we ask you to leave?"

I'm so mad. This is ridiculous. Horns start to sporadically blow around us, making me raise my voice.

"You all but did ask me to leave." My eyes connect with Cole's. "*You* walked me to the door. Told me to leave the shirt on the bed. Nobody said anything when I said there wasn't a reason for me to stay…that was your cue, dickheads."

Christopher steps in, turning toward me, trying for privacy.

"Is there something I should know? Did you date one of these guys?" He chuckles nervously, adding, "Or a couple of them because they said *we...*"

I brush my newly acquired hot girl revenge bangs from my face as I let out a whoosh of a breath.

"Not now, Christopher. You'll need a drink...or two, before I explain."

Reed smirks, pushing poor Christopher back to his place.

"Christopher, get fucked. Also, I like your hair, sunshine."

A growl rips from my throat. "I don't care." *Lies.*

Reed grins with that "up to trouble" look he gets as he keeps his eyes on me, raising his voice.

"Christopher, I can understand your confusion. Let me explain for our Samantha. I don't know if you know, but my sunshine here is a huge slut. Massive." Reed smiles down at me, and I try my level best not to do it back. So he keeps talking, "She's got a body count like Mortal Combat. We'd probably be hard-pressed to fit them all in this room. So four guys was a cakewalk. The only problem is we're not done."

Chris pipes up to defend my honor, saying, "Don't speak to her like that," but my sister pats his shoulder, interjecting, "It's all right, Chrissy, she likes it. And him."

I shake my head, confused as I push Reed back. *Did he say, we're not done?*

My hands are suddenly sweaty, so I wipe them down my cobalt blue gown before I swallow and try to put some heat behind my words.

"I answered your question. Now answer mine. Why are you here?"

Reed draws his bottom lip between his teeth before I feel his fingers lift my chin.

"We did. *You* weren't listening. We're asking you to leave with us."

My heart is beating too fast. And I'm feeling dizzy. Or maybe I just wish I'd pass out to escape this moment.

Jace steps in, blocking Christopher, who tries to interject again, drawing my attention, but my sister smacks his shoulder.

"Read the room, dummy. This isn't your moment. *You* are the supporting cast. Don't worry, I'll let you hit it later. Because I think that's my date over there making out with that guy."

We all look in the direction she's pointing before Jace places his hand on my waist, his soulful eyes doing all the damage he's intending.

"We like you, Samantha. And we want you. We're fucking idiots for not telling you that, but there was shit we needed to work out. Negotiations so to speak."

I brush Jace's hand away, looking at each of these gorgeous tuxedo-clad men. I stop on Cole, noticing the faint bruise around his eye. His jaw tenses, but he winks.

"What can I say, negotiations were intense." He starts toward me. "Because they were about something we all feel equally passionate about...*someone* we all want very much."

I stare up at his face, at the stubble on his chin, wishing I could feel it between my legs. The truth finally bubbles over.

"But I don't want another weekend. I want a chance at forever. And that's unrealistic."

"Wait...she dated all of them...at the same time?" Christopher blurts.

"Shhh," my sister counters. "Supporting character, remember?"

People begin to cheer, noisemakers swirling, the sound bouncing off the walls as they yell *ten*.

"We were one weekend and one weekend only," I yell. "That's what you said."

Nine.

Reed comes to my side, taking my hand. "Sunshine, when are you going to realize we always want what you want?"

Eight.

Jace sweeps my hair off my shoulder, staring back with pleading eyes. "Say yes, cutie."

Seven.

I'm shaking my head. "This will be doomed from the start. What are we supposed to do? All date?"

Six.

Alec cradles my face. "Why not? We're in to see where it goes if you are."

Five.

My heart is racing. The guys are surrounding me. Waiting for me to say something.

Four.

But if I say yes—it's too complicated. Too hard to navigate in the real world. Sooner or later, someone will get jealous. Or what if I fall for one of them more than the others?

Three.

I don't want to have my heart broken. Let alone by four guys.

Two

But if I say no…

…I wake up tomorrow without them.

"Yes. I say yes."

One.

I yell it over the music, barely able to get it out before I'm attacked. Balloons and confetti fall around us as kisses cover my face, neck, and hands. I laugh, trying to get my bearings, and like the anchor he is, Cole puts his hand around my throat, locking my eyes on his.

"The shiner was the price I paid to be first."

His lips crash down on mine, and everything around us stops existing. And right there at that moment, surrounded by the guys I'm falling for, my tomorrow begins.

epilogue

. . .

one glorious year later.

"**D**inner," I call out, bending over to open the
oven.

The smell of my homemade lasagna wafts
through the air, putting a smile on my face. Because it's
their favorite, and since we're back at the cabin for some
pre-Christmas fun, I figured I'd pull out all the stops.

My brows furrow because I don't hear the heavy footsteps I usually hear when I mention food or sex. I'm just
about to turn around and yell for them again when music
starts to play over the surround sound. And not just any
music. It's that damn Chipmunk song.

I scream-laugh, covering my face with my oven mitt as
I turn around.

"I am not stripping to this again, you weirdos."

But my mouth shuts. Because my eyes almost pop out
of my head.

Standing in the middle of the room are Jace, Reed, Alec, and Cole—wearing only boxer briefs and Santa hats. All of their delicious muscles are on display, beckoning for my tongue.

This never gets old. Ever.

They start dancing around, calling me to join them. So I do. Because why wouldn't I? This year's been unexpected. We've faced down side-eyes, angry fathers—*mine*—and curious questions. But at the end of the day, when the lights go out, it was always us. And that's all that matters.

I take off my apron, leaving me topless and in only my underwear as I saunter out into the room, lifting my arms to join their impromptu dance party.

Jace sweeps me up into his embrace, kissing my cheek before putting me down so Reed can sandwich me. Our bodies move like lovers, swaying and grinding. Cole tips my chin up, making me lean sideways as he kisses me.

"Wanna let us tangle you up in some tinsel?"

I straighten, biting my lip, wrapping my hand around Reed's neck who's behind me. Jace dives down, taking my nipple in his mouth as I look over at Alec.

I love you, he mouths, taking a seat in a chair, legs open as he rubs his cock.

"I love you," I breathe out to all my guys as lips touch my neck, and someone puts their hand down the front of my underwear.

Who knew a year ago I would make a naughty deal for the weekend and find four loves of my life?

But that's what happened. And if that isn't a Christmas miracle, I don't know what is.

THANK YOU FOR READING TANGLED IN TINSEL. SIGN UP FOR my newsletter on **www.trilinapucci.com,** so you don't miss the extended epilogue. It's sure to get you a spot on the naughty list!

What you should read next...

Based on which guy is your favorite.

Reed is so Daddy:

Hillcrest Prep

TRAVEL BACK TO THE PLACE THAT MADE HIM, HILLCREST PREP, AND MEET THE NEWEST BATCH OF RICH, ARROGANT CHARMERS. THINK GOSSIP GIRL MEETS CRUEL INTENTIONS MIXED WITH A WHOLE OF ANGST.

I need another tatted Boston bad boy:

Star-Crossed Duet

WELL, JACE ISN'T REALLY A BAD BOY, BUT CALDER IS... THINK DARK ROMEO AND JULIET, JUST ADD MAFIA. YOU WILL DEDICATE YOUR LIFE TO HIM. HE'S ELITE, AND THIS DUET MIGHT WRECK YOU IN THE BEST WAY.

Tell me I'm a good girl, Cole, while Alec watches:

A Sinful Dark Mafia Series

IF CONTROLLING DOMS ARE YOUR THING, RUN, DON'T WALK TO MY MAFIA SERIES. THREE ITALIAN CHICAGO BROTHERS WHO OWN A SEX CLUB CALLED CHURCH. IT'S HIGH SPICE AND BIG FAMILY DINNERS.

acknowledgments

It takes a whole village to create a book, and I love my village.

Firstly, and in no particular order, thank you to Gretchen, Katie, Jen, and Serena for listening to me endlessly about the plot and reading and re-reading chapter after chapter.

Thank you to all the bloggers and influencers, especially my review team and promotional crew, for all the ways you hype me up and cheer me on. I adore you beyond words!

Big shout-out to my friend, Abby. Without your encouragement, I'm not sure a Trilina romcom would exist. I owe you at least a dinner, now.

And my finally to my *sisters in christ*—you the baddest b's there are. You were with me for every word, and you kept me going when I couldn't see my way through *the scene*. Here's to summer writing retreats and lake days in the future.

about the author

Trilina is a USA Today Best-selling Author who loves cupcakes and bourbon.

When she isn't writing steamy love stories, she can be found devouring Netflix with her husband, Anthony, and their three kiddos. Pucci's journey into writing started impulsively. She wanted to check off a box on her bucket list, but what began as wish-fulfillment has become incredibly fulfilling. Now she can't see her life without her characters, her readers, and this community.

She's known for being a trope-defier, writing outside of the box and creating fictional worlds that her readers never want to leave.

Connect with Trilina and stay up to date.

copyright

Made in United States
Orlando, FL
16 December 2022

26767783R00157